FIRST LOVE

Mikhail Roshchin

FIRST LOVE

A Novel

Translated from the Russian by
Antonina W. Bouis

Marion Boyars
New York · London

First published in the United States and Great Britain in 1991 by
Marion Boyars Publishers
26 East 33rd Street, New York, NY 10016
24 Lacy Road, London SW15 1NL

Distributed in the United States and Canada by
Rizzoli International Publications, New York

Distributed in Australia by
Wild and Woolley, Glebe, NSW

Library of Congress Cataloging-in-Publication Data
Roshchin, Mikhail.
First love/Mikhail Roshchin: translated from the Russian by
Antonina W. Bouis.
I. Title.
PG3485.6.S5F57 1991
891.73′44—dc20

British Library Cataloguing in Publication Data
Roshchin, Mikhail
First love.
I. Title
891.7344
ISBN 0–7145–2932–X Cloth

Typeset in Bodoni and 11½/13½pt Baskerville by
Ann Buchan (Typesetters), Middx
Printed and bound in Great Britain by Itchen Printers Limited, Southampton.

FIRST LOVE

I was sixteen, still at school, and I fell in love with a teacher.

Here's my school, in a narrow, sloping Moscow alley. You have to walk past the Khiva, the green 'Hussar's' beer hall, the little white house, and then through the schoolyard.

The Khiva is a bath house; the beer hall was called 'Hussar's' because of the barmaid Nura, who was as big as a horse and had a mustache. The two-story white building stood apart, with a tile roof, and had a foreign, Dutch look. The schoolyard was cramped, dusty, trampled, with tall old poplars growing in it. Beyond the poplars you could see a typical school building of pale gray brick, with lots of windows in its four stories.

It stands there now as it did thirty years ago, even though everything around it has changed. They tore down the bath house, they tore down the two-story buildings, and now the school, which used to be the tallest structure in the alley, is hemmed in by new high rises and long 'endless' apartment houses.

Everything has vanished; only memory remains.

In fifth grade Vitka Muravyov whose nickname was 'Ant' (we learned from our English lessons that this is what his name meant in English) climbed the mountain of coal in the yard of the Khiva and discovered that in the evenings it gave a view of the women's wash room. We used to climb up and watch. Naked women with wet hair moved in the murky light, as if in an underwater kingdom.

In sixth grade Mishka Provadkin, a foul-mouthed thief who was held back for the third time — he had lost a leg under a trolley when he was stealing raisins from a freight train and fell off — led us into 'the Hussars' for the first time. He bounced on his crutch and used it to clear a path for us. 'Go in, snotnoses!' he shouted. 'No sweat! It's on me!' Nura the Hussar — her gigantic height and black mustache were astonishing — berated us for being minors, but poured out Mishka's orders, giving us heavy, chipped mugs that looked bitten around the rims. The beer was a good draft brew; 'unspoiled' the local men called it. The laborers were there, faces boiled red in the baths, juicily blowing the heavy foam off onto the black floor. 'No sweat!' Mishka shouted and hopped agilely, crutch under his arm, two mugs in his hand. 'No sweat, little guys! Drink! Drink, Pioneers, sons of the working class!'

In seventh grade we were drawn to the white house. The three Shub sisters lived there: Tanya Shub, Anya Shub, and Natasha Shub. Each spring in turn one of the sisters blossomed. They were the prettiest girls of our youth, and they resembled young ladies: Tanya and Anya were blond with big blue eyes, like dolls, and Natasha was dark, with a black braid and agate eyes. The sisters played piano, and in the spring the cultivated sounds of music reached the Khiva through the open Dutch window filled with cyclamen, and our hooligan hearts melted with lofty emotions.

Sometimes we played volleyball behind the white house, and if Tanya (or Anya, or especially Natasha) threw the ball three times in a row only to you, everyone exchanged knowing looks, and you were filled with pride and embarrassment.

In those days we were separated, boys and girls in different schools, like students in pre-revolutionary Gymnasiums or Lycées. The girls wore a uniform which was almost like the old Gymnasium one, and the relationships that formed were of the Gymnasium type; mannered and alienated. Even though there was nothing of the Gymnasium about us.

At the beginning of summer the alley, the bath house, the school and its yard were filled with fluffy cottonwood from the old poplars: these noiseless blizzards swirled through the classrooms, everyone had itchy noses, and we wrote our final exams in a lacework of fluff. Layers of cottony seeds collected along the floors. Sometimes someone would slide off his seat and throw a lighted match, and the flame would run merrily as if along a trail of gunpowder. Then the teacher would screech and jump up, and the class would scream raucously — anything to break up the lesson. But we were finishing eighth grade, we were grown up, and even our jokes were different now.

We were on the fourth floor at the top. The Khiva, the white house and the red roofs were all below us, including the lopsided little house of our favorite teacher, Valentina Ivanovna. It was right across the street, and when we were on the first and second floors, its windows looked directly at us. Valentina Ivanovna had a large family, a small salary, lots of cares and chores, and she was not surrounded by the usual mystery that surrounds teachers. (Who was she? How did she live?) She would force open the double-framed windows in winter or summer, one after the other, and shout, 'Tanya! Bring my watch, I forgot it!' or, 'Mama! I left the laundry boiling! Stir it!' When we were in fifth and sixth grade we'd lean halfway out the windows during recess and shout so the whole alley could hear, 'Ta-a-nya! Bring my watch!'

Seventh grade was the divide then. After seventh grade, half the kids left for vocational school or jobs. During the war almost everyone had missed a year or two, so there were fifteen- and sixteen-year-olds in seventh grade. There were fewer and fewer of us; say, three seventh graders, two eighth graders, only one in ninth grade, and one in tenth grade. Tenth grade was the pinnacle, the elite, practically an autonomous state.

When we were promoted to eighth grade, the tenth grade, the graduating class, seemed particularly special. They were serious men with mustaches. The difference of a year or two is never felt in later life as strongly as it is in school. The gap between us in eighth grade and those in the tenth was like that between earth and heaven. Of course, they really were smart guys, each of whom knew what he wanted.

When they — some in ties, some in fully adult coats or suits, with heavy briefcases (we didn't even carry briefcases, we'd just shove a textbook and our notebooks inside our coat, but enough of that) — stood by the school before classes, smoking freely, and speaking importantly about their important affairs, we whisked past them, like students before professors.

They walked differently (they didn't run), were late differently (without demeaning themselves with lies or by hiding in attics and toilets), joked openly (without giggling, blushing, or whispering) with our young teachers and the Pioneer leader Zoya, and broke fives and tens at the cafeteria (instead of counting copper coins). They were leaders at school meetings, and we voted for their proposals. While we finished up, disrupted lessons and got carried away with ourselves and our fiery friendships — we were a crazy and fun-loving class — they gnawed on the granite of scholarships.

They left school like kings: thirteen of the sixteen students received medals: it was unheard of! In the autumn all of them went to college, and not just any old ones. They went to the physics-mathematics, physics-technology, and philosophy institutes.

They put up a marble board in school with their names inscribed in gold, and their example, their glory, was pounded not only into our heads but also the heads of those who came after us.

I wanted to grow up and be in tenth grade as soon as possible.

But first I had ninth, a whole school year, ahead of me.

Why hadn't I noticed her before? How was it possible? We had met at school hundreds of times; she had been an assistant in our seventh-grade exams, pretending not to notice when we used cribs. Like everyone else, she was given a nickname: Blondie (rather gentle among cruel school nicknames), which was the brand name of an expensive vodka with a white cap. That was because of her pale white, silky hair, white face, and light eyes. In general her sleek head, her slender and always bare neck and her sloping shoulders made her figure resemble the shape of a bottle. Her two brothers, the twins Pavka and Slavka, were with us in the seventh grade. I even knew where she lived: in Maly Khivinsky Alley, five minutes from school, in an old three-story building. Its top two floors were faced with old-fashioned green ceramic tiles with white birds: that's why it was called the Bird House.

Maybe I had noticed her. Or maybe I had changed, but that day she paid attention to me and thereby attracted my attention.

It was September the first, we were running toward school and crowding in front of it in the morning sun. School was school, and the morning was the kind of morning you have on September the first. But still, that day always seemed new. You run, and your heart pounds: you're going to see everybody, it's going to start! Everything will be different, a different class, new subjects, a different life.

We gathered, greeting everyone with shouts of joy: we had missed each other, had perhaps even matured a little over the summer. We shook hands, slapped shoulders, 'Hey, guys, look at Ant, look!'

Little Ant had grown a just perceptible mustache. Our stern Captain (Stepa Serabekyan) was clean shaven and he regarded our tussling with condemnation and, as usual, we could expect new sharp ideas from him and opinions like no one else's. Sanya Yablochkin was back from Germany where he had visited his father, the general (watch, cigarette lighter, foreign cigarettes), and he was acting a bit condescending, as if he knew something that we never would. My friend Voka showed me a picture he kept in his hands of a pouty-lipped and sleepy-looking girl: 'I'll tell you later, you'll die!' Fat Zheka Borisov was even fatter, and glasses glimmered on his face.

I had also changed, grown taller and thinner, my hair sun-bleached and longer. I purposely didn't get a haircut. I was wearing a new jacket with a zipper and new shoes. I had been staying in a village up north and learned to mow with a scythe and work a thresher. I had herded and washed horses. Grandmother and I had dried half a sack of mushrooms. I read a lot that summer: I was stunned by Flaubert's *Salambo* and I gulped down Sienckewicz. 'Listen, have you read *Quo Vadis*? How about you? Who's read *Quo Vadis*?'

Looking at me with his yellow, marbled eyes, only Captain Stepa said, 'Well, I've read it,' and looked ready to enter into an argument about it with me.

More people came, the school was chattering and lining up. Margosha, our class supervisor, came; a homey, funny woman in a feathered hat. We surrounded her and all of us turned out to be taller than her by a head (except for Ant).

They kept trying to line up the students. The school smelled of fresh paint, the sun shone in the washed windows (not a single one broken), the brass of the puny school band glinted, and the musicians were all wearing white shirts and red ties. A group of idlers, together with the parents of the little kids, stood across the street. People were staring out of the windows of Valentina Ivanovna's house.

But then the principal, the teachers, district representatives and the parents' committee went up on the porch in a motley group, looking as if they were a tribune. We stood below.

'Look at Chichkin, look!' The buzzing went up and down the lines. 'And look at the Nose!'

It was the first time in our lives that we saw our principal, Ivan Mikhailovich, not wearing an army uniform but civilian clothes, a rather light suit. A starched collar and a new tie propped up his neck. The Nose (vice principal Ivan Ivanovich) was also brilliant in a summer jacket, though it was baggy and the pockets were soiled.

On the porch were familiar figures and faces: the physics teacher Golubchik (the smoker was still alive!) and the tubercular technical drawing teacher, Fried Pipette, as shy as a maiden. Then there was the sly smile and mysterious Japanese hairdo of Raisa Yakovlevna. Beyond, behind these, was a solid flower bed of the younger teachers, the ones who taught the lower grades.

'Who's that?' I asked Voka, who was standing behind me in line, and even as he answered in surprise, I understood: it was Blondie.

Voka said, 'Who? That's Blondie.'

Of course, I had barely recognized her: she was young, her hair brushed back, with a bun on her nape, cheerful. Striped dress with a broad sailor's collar. Slender. White faced even after the summer. Her lips lightly made up, like all the women. Blondie.

She was whispering with another young teacher, Lubov Petrovna, her girl friend, both were giggling like girls.

The noise was not abating, Chichkin's glasses flashed, and he raised a hand. In the other, he held a piece of paper with his speech on it. Really, he was hard to recognize. But then he roared, 'Silence!' and a sigh of relief went through the rows, 'It's him! Chichkin!'

The principal looked behind him again — the teachers hadn't quite stopped talking and laughing, either — and straining his voice, he began reading the speech. We stopped listening immediately, from his first words.

I couldn't take my eyes off the porch. Was that really her, Blondie, Anna Nikolayevna, our teacher? Why hadn't I noticed what she was like before? Of course, Anna Nikolayevna, Annyusha, Blondie, 4B on the first floor, next to the cloakroom. In the mornings you run in and she's in the doorway, gathering up her small fry. . .

In the lines to my right and left young bass voices were talking, eighth-grader Kuptsov, hiding behind people's backs, was mimicking Chichkin, Voka was snorting into the back of my head. I didn't pay any attention. I was staring at one thing.

And a minute later our eyes met.

I swear, it happened at that moment. Her eyes opened in surprise, as if asking, 'What are you doing?' Then open fear flickered in them. She looked away and down, while I. . .

Chichkin moved his mouth silently, then the band moved its brass instruments silently, the school building shook and stood still. I had been somewhere else and returned. Far, far away. A wave had struck me, carried me off and brought me back.

Later, recalling that day a hundred times, going over every detail, Anna Nikolayevna and I agreed that it was that first look which determined everything. We were both right.

But perhaps, even more important was what happened later. Anna Nikolayevna began to blush. She glowed, blazed, turned as red as the 'Welcome' banner behind her.

I had a flash: school hallways, recess, our group leaning against the wall, and a young teacher happening by, running the gauntlet. And suddenly she begins to blush. For no reason. She wants to run, but her dignity won't let her, and she lowers her head, very low, and walks, poor thing, while we make fun. Somebody calls out a joke behind her.

We even used to make bets when we saw her coming, would she blush or not? No need to guess — she always did. Just made that way. You could feel sorry for her.

But now — now she was blushing for all to see, without any reason, and how! Forehead, neck, even her chest was covered with red spots in the white neckline of her dress — poor woman, her embarrassment over blushing made her blush even more.

She bent down; she began coughing, covering her mouth with a hankie; people looked at her, especially the Nose. Lubov Petrovna put an arm around her in fear and looked sharply down the lines, guessing that the threat was coming from there, from us.

'Look at yours, look at her!' Voka whispered behind me and giggled.

I jabbed him with my elbow.

What was happening to me! I felt faint, my head was blazing. I didn't understand yet, but I felt it had happened. Important, powerful. Something I had never felt. I felt sorry for her. I was ashamed of myself, afraid to look up: I thought the whole school had turned to look at me. And at the same time, victorious, joyful. Was it possible? Me and that young but grown-up woman, a teacher? Impossible! But I had seen her eyes, I had! Why had she blushed that way?

At that moment I didn't think about it, but actually there have been such incidents. They said, for instance, that there had been something between beautiful Pioneer leader Zoya and Vladik Figurkov, whom I had described, from the tenth grade. But Figurkov was a giant of a man, a volleyball star, athletic, calm and haughty. And Zoya was a Pioneer leader, not a teacher.

Last year there had been another story in our district: about a tenth-grade girl and a literature teacher from a girls' school. That there had been a big scandal, the girl almost had a baby by him. But he had a wife, or didn't have a wife, but wouldn't marry her. Something like that. Something ugly and scandalous.

No wonder the Nose once forbade us from going to a dance at the girls' school, saying, 'You can't go because you will develop an unhealthy interest in the opposite sex!' ('Healthy!' shouted Voka excitedly.)

In the meantime our assembly continued. There were more and more speeches; from the factory whose personnel volunteered time for the school and had done our repairs, from the district Komsomol, from the parents' committee. After every speech the band played a raggedy fanfare. Kids were bored and started fooling around in the lines. Kuptsov continued his imitations of the speakers. The fifth graders shot paper clips at the band.

A Party representative began talking. We made rude noises. A clean little Pioneer from fourth grade thanked everyone in his clarion voice and promised that we would all get only A's and B's this year. At that came a volley of paper clips, one hit him in the nose, and he burst into tears.

Voka behind me was dying of laughter, poking me in the back, but for the first time in my life the general hilarity went on without me. When I had the nerve to look at the porch once more, I saw Anna Nikolayevna still pressing the hankie to her lips, not looking around, and her face was now whiter than her white hair.

And I. . . I only wanted just one thing: another time! Again! Another look! It had happened! I wasn't mistaken!

The Nose realized it was time to end the ceremony. Another minute and the school would be standing on its head. He whispered to Chichkin. He nodded, raised his hand, barked that the solemn assembly dedicated to the start of the new school year was over. There was applause, shouts of 'Hurray!' Everything was in motion, the band belatedly started up some tune, and the conductor sadly waved his hand to stop them. Some saw his gesture and stopped, others didn't understand and went on blowing, creating total chaos. The teachers broke up and went down the steps to their classes.

I saw Anna hurry, her striped dress flashed by me, a fat parent gave her a bouquet, which she accepted with thanks, but distractedly, it seemed to me. I saw the tension in her smile. And I knew very well that she was terrified of looking in my direction.

Once again there was talk, lining up, laughter. Margosha's feathered hat flickered here and there, then the electric bell — another innovation — rang in the bowels of the empty school. In the past Auntie Galya, a nurse's aide, used to go from floor to floor ringing a brass hand bell that came from a small ship. Chichkin, all smiles, raised a finger so that everyone would listen to the marvel of the new bell.

It was time to move into the school.

And without orders or shouts the noise died down, faded, and people moved off together in an orderly way. Something had happened in a single minute. They stopped fooling around, giggling and hitting. The adults grew serious, and their genuine seriousness was passed on to us. The lines straightened. And all eyes were on a single event.

I picked up on the general tension and forgot for a moment about Anna Nikolayevna and myself.

Actually nothing special was happening. Simply, and in accordance with the traditional ritual, the first graders were about to enter the building. They were being led to the porch by a new young teacher, with reddish hair and freckles — she was glowing, in the center of attention.

Usually the sight of the first graders' march elicited tenderness, smiles and a mocking respect. From the back you could see their uniformly shaved heads, whitish from the barber's razors, and their white collars. They twisted their necks, looking over at their mothers and grandmothers. Their new satchels almost touched the ground. The stalks of gladioli they were bringing for the teacher stuck out in all directions. The teacher bustled around them like a brood hen, whispering, bending over tenderly. By now she had the first one by the hand and was leading him into the school.

It was as familiar as two times two and probably would not have created such tension if not for one circumstance. All our classes were lined up, the whole school, and there were a lot of us, over a thousand people. Each grade had several classes: five second grades, and five thirds, and five fourths, and fifths, and sixths. There were four seventh grades: Seven A, Seven B, Seven C, and Seven D. (The older grades didn't count.) But this year we had only one first grade class. Just one. And its line was noticeably shorter than the others. Just One A.

The freckled teacher gave the order for them to move, and they did: clumsily, falling behind or bumping into their partners, dragging their satchels on the steps, still looking back. The old women on the sidewalk moaned a bit and the men frowned. Ivan Mikhailovich pulled off his glasses and wiped his eyes with an unfolded handkerchief. Auntie Galya, wearing a white polka-dotted scarf for the holiday, held the door open and nodded painfully, as if bowing at the waist. The boys poured through the door and did not understand, did not suspect why they were accorded such a silent and sorrowful respect.

These were the boys born in nineteen forty-two.

That's why there were so few of them.

About a month later I was sitting with Anna one evening in the brightly lit and empty classroom of Five A. I had led the Pioneer meeting for her class and we had let the kids leave but we stayed on, talking. Auntie Galya looked in to clean up, but waved a hand at us, 'Sit! Sit! I have lots of work to do in the other rooms!'

Anna was telling me about her fiancé, Lieutenant Orest Chestnokov. He had been mobilized at the end of the war, having barely finished college and had been killed two months before Victory Day in a troop train headed for the front. She was eighteen. They hadn't had time to get married.

My father had not come back from the front either. Not only that, he was missing in action. In those days it was considered worse than being killed. (Though what could be **worse?**) And my mother, also a young woman, was left alone. Listening to Anna, I thought of my mother. Perhaps for the first time I saw her as a woman who had been left without a husband instead of as a mother. Strange.

But we still had hope: Everyone who had family 'Missing in Action' waited many years for them to return. And there were instances when they did return.

Voka filled me in on his summer story. 'I'm only telling you, no one else, understand?' And he was winking and laughing, as if about to tell me something funny. I believed him and I didn't believe him. Voka was capable of fibbing, even though we all knew that girls liked his catlike face. At school dances, when we played post office, the mailmen brought him loads of letters: 'From number 17 for number 4!' 'From number 39 for number 4!' 'From number 22 for number 4!' Of course, once you got a good look at number 17 or 22, you'd laugh: they were all stupid girls with fat legs or pimples. Red and sweaty with excitement, they giggled like little girls and sent stupid letters! 'Fie, Voka!' Sanya Yablochkin would say (he was on the ball). 'Fie! They're mediocre, all mediocre!' But Voka would reply, 'Sir, what do you know about it?' And he would sort the notes, write replies, all excited and sweaty himself, setting dates, running to meet them, lying and shouting, 'Let's drink to our conquests!'

But what he told me seemed like the truth.

As usual, he had spent the summer at a dacha near Moscow. He hung around with a crowd of girls and boys by a pond, swam, rode his bicycle, played soccer in an empty field. What else is there to do in the summer? In the evening they danced to the radio placed in a window so it could be heard. Everyone was in love with someone — that was the atmosphere. . . I had visited Voka at the dacha and as he told his story, I could picture the pond and the house, the crowd and the trampled ground where they danced. The commuter train turned round there and would suddenly blind the dancers with its long headlights, illuminating both them and the cloud of dust at their feet.

When it rained they would gather indoors where there were always the two brassy sisters, or the terrific guy, or the young women, older than the rest. There were never any parents, and the room was large and empty and there was also a terrace and dark corners, and nothing to eat, and the kids swiped stuff from home, some bringing bread, others sausage. You could smoke, shout, sing, play records, play cards, flirt, play spin the bottle, and even chip in for wine. Someone would run down in the rain to the station canteen to get it — it was fun, barefoot in the mud, raincoat over your head — or take a bike across the wet grass and splash through the puddles. Two bottles for fifteen people and loads of fun, laughter, freedom! The important thing was that you could do everything that was forbidden, everyone was a pal and understood you, and no one would bark that you were still wet behind the ears. . . Lights out, candles lit, the same record over and over again, dancing close and slow. The couples would grow quiet, freeze at the end of each dance, the girls looking away. The next dance starts as soon as the stylus is moved back to the beginning of the record, and everyone waits, relaxing their embrace, but not separating, and you dance with the same girl again, and again and again.

You've been exchanging glances with her for a long time, at the pond, you push her in the water, in the general horsing around you accidentally brush against her breast, grab her legs underwater when you dive — just a game! Coming back from the pond, you make a point of carrying her on the handlebars of your bike, in front of you. Oh! that bike! Your lips almost touch the back of her head, which smells of the river, the breeze blows her hair against your cheeks, her back pressing soft and warm against your chest, and your right arm keeps touching her breast. Ten minutes ago out of the corner of your eye you saw her take off her bathing suit: already wearing the dress which stuck to her wet body, she lowered the suit down to her feet and trampled it slightly first, with one foot, then the other, barely keeping her balance.

She sits sideways on the bike, her bare knees pressed innocently together and hanging over the road in that position, blind you with their roundness, their nutty tan. A splotch of iodine, you had put it on a cut on her right leg last night: you smeared the glass stick on the cut while she sat on the porch, lifting her sun dress on to her thigh, saying 'ouch' more than necessary until you bent real close and blew on it the way you blow on a baby's wound.

And then the hay was mowed. The peasants cut grass in every ravine, ditch and bank of the pond, the sharp aroma of grass sap was everywhere. And the next day, the smell of grass drying in the sun. Dew fell, a crimson moon came out, and you're sitting on the edge of a ditch, behind the village, under over-hanging berries. The horned bicycle gleams next to you on the ground, your hand is inside her blouse, she cringes, but not a word, it's been an hour without a word and then another, only the pressing, hot faces, chills, inevitability. . .

Voka climbed into the window of his dacha at three in the morning with all due caution, but his father came into his room wearing long johns, flashing a light not really necessary at dawn, in his face, and said, 'Is that you, you idiot? Who gave you life, me or Maupassant? I'll burn that Maupassant to hell!' Voka's mother sobbed in the next room, 'He's going to be ruined! Ruined!'

About three days later all the hay was swept into stacks, you could fall into them — sit for hours under a stack and then lie down together. 'She never said a word,' Voka recounted, 'I'd try to mutter something, it was somehow embarrassing, but her . . . like wood! A log!. . . We were lying down already, all that stuff, wouldn't let me kiss her, mumbling no with her mouth shut, shaking her head, and I thought: I can't do anything, and then I thought, yes I can, since she's not saying anything. . '

What happened in the hay was repeated two more times, and by then they almost hated each other, avoided each other, didn't look into each other's eyes in broad daylight, and it all ended just as silently, without explanations.

Of course, Voka only told me the part about how it ended and how brief it had been later. At first, particularly when he was showing me the photo, it seemed that it was still going on. Especially since Voka still went to the dacha once or twice in September. 'I'm going to the dacha tomorrow,' he would say with a wink. 'Want to come?' I just snorted in reply. All the same, I really wanted to have a look at his Natasha; I was drawn as if to a keyhole.

After his story (there were two or three more details that never left my mind and which I even dreamed about) Voka became somehow repulsive to me, even physically. Something was wrong. No wonder he hid how it had ended. If Captain Stepa had heard him, he would have given him a scornful look.

Voka had crossed the line, broken the vow. He had gone where we all were drawn, but we fought it, we were winning. We were like maidens and were waiting for Love. And now what? Really, what an idiot! We ended up looking like fools while he wrapped us around his finger.

I was also jealous: my best friend had been stolen. He had been held in a stranger's arms and then returned. But who had been returned? And with what?

Despite myself, I envied him. How had that bum managed to do it all so easily? He had moved away from me, but strangely, not down, not to the side, but up. I didn't even know how to treat him. As if he were an adult and I were still a child. As if I had always been smart and he stupid, and suddenly it turns out that I'm the fool!

And I also thought: how will Voka live now? With that open secret, that exposed world of Woman? Why hadn't anything changed in him? I thought *everything* would change. But Voka was still Voka: merry, talkative, the life of the party, giggling, getting A's. What would happen if they found out about it at school?

Adults fear *it* all their lives, like fire. They think we shouldn't know anything about it. And since we're not supposed to, then we don't. Not knowing is moral, and knowing is immoral. And out of fear we pretend not to know. Hypocrisy.

We'd already read a hundred novels, seen a hundred movies, studied sculptures and paintings in museums. Secretly in libraries we'd leafed through encyclopedias and heavy volumes with chilling titles like *Man and Woman*. And way back when, in sixth grade, I guess, when we used to bring small trophies to show and trade — crosses, coins, penknives, bullets, insignia — under a desk, in someone's hands there would be German officer's brown pictures on stiff cardboard: photographs of something wild for children's eyes.

How could we not know? What else do you do exposed to neighbors, sisters, mothers, the drunken woman by the beer hall, divorcees, gossip, brawls, weddings and evening stories in the yard told by Zhora, the veteran, nicknamed Snot? What else do you do, knowing about the war? There's nothing sharper than a child's observing eye and a child's listening ear. What else can you do with your own body, so frightening with its uncontrollable processes?

Everyone thinks that children know nothing and shouldn't know anything. But it's very easy to check: just remember what and when you knew or saw for yourself. At what age?

It would be strange to admit that lies suit everyone and the truth is better hidden.

Or is shame more valuable than the truth?. . .

In the morning we met at school.

To see her, see her for just a minute. Otherwise it felt as if I wouldn't be able to live through the day! All my thoughts were about that.

Chichkin and the Nose were astonished by the change in me: I was not late, not sick, didn't play hooky (almost), I was hanging around the school all day. The teachers couldn't get it, Margosha sniff–sniff–sniffed, the class laughed. I was happy to run for the register in the teachers' lounge, or for chalk, or to wet the eraser pad. I'd disappear for five minutes or so, and then reappear, holding my panting breath.

For all that I practically flunked the quarter and was starting to fail the next one.

. . . People with satchels and briefcases, big and small, were running from all sides in the dark of a winter's morning to the school door. The small ones were dragged by the hand. We met at one point in space, like bees in a hive. The heavy door swung back and forth. The ice was chipped away from the porch and the steps were sanded. All the windows blazed with yellow light, as if at night, and the light fell in squares on the trampled snow.

By tradition, the teachers waited for us in the entrance hall. It was cold and noisy. Some wore shawls, others had their coats flung over their shoulders. It was drafty, and dirty snow melted on the tile floor, even though we stamped our feet on the hemp rugs. Where was she?

In the doorways, the corridors and the cloakroom came the first morning exercises, the stupid school tussles. Hit him with your briefcase! Kick! Slap! Jab! Hop! . . . Roll into the cloakroom!

'No running!'

As usual, Ivan Mikhailovich, in his everyday costume of army shirt and boots, paced the landing on the stairway, like a captain on the bridge. To keep us from running through the halls, we were forced to line up by class. Chichkin loved lines, people standing to attention. 'Attention!' he roared during breaks. 'No running! Halt! What's your name? *Qui-et!*'

The Nose lurked by the bannister, holding a pile of registers and mysterious folders tied with ribbons, pressing them down with his elbow while he made a note in his book of transgressors. He shivered in the draft, his famous nose snuffling, but he stayed there, seeing everything, missing nothing.

Behind them on the landing was a silver-painted bust on a red calico pedestal. Beneath it stood potted plants, without flowers. Each pot was wrapped in foil. Above it, dusty banners with tassels crisscrossed.

And we broiled and boiled below, like a windblown sea.

'*Qui-et!* No running!'

'H'lo Iv'Mikhail'ch!'

From far away, still in the door, I saw her body, her smooth platinum head. She was huddling in a shawl, hunched over, her face pale and sleepy. What! Was she sick? She shouted mechanically at her class, lined them up — now she had Five A, horrible kids — and talked with Lubov Petrovna or some other teacher. They were probably talking about shopping, planning who had a free period in her schedule and could run to the store in the middle of the day. Or she just stood there, shouting, saying hello, answering her students' questions, but not really present, huddled in her shawl.

I saw her and my heart started pounding. Look,

look at me!. . . I've run in without my coat, red with cold (if you're not wearing a coat you're not considered late, you could have simply been held up in the cloakroom, and besides, it's cool not to wear a coat!). She looked at me meekly and then averted her gaze, her expression not changing, and she continued lining up the kids. The Nose or anyone else had nothing to notice.

But I was quick enough to see something: embarrassment, a light, light blush on her cheek. 'Yes, I see you, I see everything, I'm glad, but please pass quickly, don't slow down.'

If she was with Lubov and she saw me, then Lubov, even though not a word had been said, watched her eyes and turned to me. And then back to her. Anna Nikolayevna shrugged slightly: as if to say, what's it to me?. . . Then both laughed a bit.

Go ahead and laugh! Big deal, a tenth-grader with a crush on a teacher, he's not the first! But I'm not blind, either!

'Greetings, Lubov Petrovna!'

'Greetings,' Lubov responded with a laugh. 'Want to catch a cold?' And then she looked over at Anna Nikolayevna, as if it were up to her to forbid me going around without my coat.

Five A, breaking ranks, reached for me, shouting, saying hello, I waved at them, 'later, pals, later,' and ran on, shaking hands along the way with my friends. And suddenly I would slap someone on the back or throw my hat or jump up with outstretched hand: a piece of wiring hangs down from the ceiling in the hallway, left over from the repairs, and we all jump there, trying to reach it.

I — love — her!

The entrance hall has to empty one minute before the bell. Woe to the latecomer!

'What's this? What's your name? Up against the wall! Write an explanation!'

'The bell, Ivan Mikhailovich!'

'Silence! Write!'

I was late. Why was I late? Mother had a day off, she overslept and didn't wake me up in time. And then she wanted me to bring in firewood, she was going to do the laundry. I talked back, she got mad. I had to go to the shed and carry in frozen logs.

'Write!' the director barks.

I made a face, settled down on the window sill, tore out a sheet from my notebook, which drove the Nose crazy, and wrote nonsense ('In accordance with Rule 6 of the school handbook, a student must come to school, clean and neat. Discovering a missing button on part of my clothing this morning, I began looking for a needle and thread. I must note that in our house finding a needle is as difficult as finding one in a haystack. . .' And so on.) I wrote and cursed myself, imagining her looking at the door until the last minute, taking her class up the stairs, lagging behind on purpose, letting kids pass on the landings, looking back at the door, at the clock. . . Damn! Now she would think something's happened to me. And me? I wouldn't be able to sit through the class.

Damned Nose read my explanation without a

smile, untied his folder, and put the page inside it with the others.

'You'll see me after school.'

'I can't after school, my grandmother. . .'

'See me after school.'

'What for? What did I do?'

'After school!'

I stared at his mug with hatred, but he didn't care! Creep! Gray cardinal! The hell with him!. . . Skinny figure, shiny suit, as if he had poured cooking oil all over it, felt boots, tie rolled up into a tube, and that nose! The nose sat on his small-featured face, a nose that belonged on an Easter Island giant. If that weren't bad enough, it was infected and swollen — the assistant principal smeared it with salves, powdered it, bandaged it and burned it, which gave it an incomparable look. Raisa Yakovlevna, pretending that she wasn't saying such a thing, once said that anyone else with a nose like that wouldn't even stick it out the door. And that was the truth. But no, it never occurred to the Nose that he might be repulsive to someone. No way! How could they manage without him? As far as he was concerned, if he missed a day at school, everything would collapse into ruins, the two great pillars would collapse: Discipline and Progress. Order before all else!

Chichkin was better. Even though he blew up, he got over it quickly. If the Nose weren't there now, he'd certainly have let us off, at least the little kids. But now we had to stand and wait, it took almost fifteen minutes.

Chichkin himself brought the latecomers to their classes. Hup, two, forward march! He ran up the stairs so that we could barely keep up, even though his belly poked out of his military shirt. (He didn't mind chasing after us down the hallways, either.) The little kids couldn't keep up at all: they panted along, eyes bulging in fear. We joked about it, but they were a pitiful sight.

'Quiet! Attention!'

He flung open the door, stepped back and rushed into the classroom. The teacher was startled, the class jumped up, banging desk lids (they were all warm and cozy and sleepy), and he pushed me in front of him and left me standing there: take a look at this miserable scoundrel, how he interrupts the lessons and breaks the rules!

'Take your seat!'

I shuffled to my seat, my back expressing guilt and obedience, while I winked at the class and made faces.

No sooner did I walk down the aisle and plonk myself down, than Chichkin was gone, marching onward.

'What happened to you?' Voka asked.

'The hell with them all! It's all the Nose's fault!'

'Quiet, quiet!' the teacher said from the board, ready to continue the lesson. 'It's bad enough you're late, without. . . So, where were we?'

'*Why don't you shut up!*' I thought. '*You keep quiet, you spectacled beetle!*' And I sat there glumly, like Lermontov's Demon, not listening and not wanting to hear.

How could I escape, what excuse could I use?. . . I turned once to Sanya, then again (he's got a watch). 'What time is it? Is it over soon?' I couldn't sit to the end of the class, I raised my hand nervously, 'Oh, I'm sorry, I didn't unplug the iron at home! Can I run down and call the neighbors?' (Actually, we didn't have a phone in our apartment block.)

School wasn't the best place for a rendezvous, but as they say, God helps lovers. All the things I did just to get a glimpse of her! I flew down the empty hallways and stairs — it was dangerous and I had to go down two flights without running into anyone. The double doors were shut, voices humming behind them, but any one of them could open at any moment.

I made it! Here was Five A! It was her lesson. I risked it and opened one side of the door. Every second counted.

Whenever a door was opened slightly during a lesson, it meant that the teacher was being called. I couldn't peek in, the kids in the first few rows would know it was me. The teacher went to the door, and the class immediately took advantage and started making a noise.

I heard her steps, I smelled the fetid air of the classroom. She stopped.

'Yagodkin! Sit down!'

She came over. I pressed my back hard against the part of the double doors which did not open. Here she was, partly in the doorway. So close! Her eyes flickered, she wasn't expecting me. She had come to the door all businesslike, annoyed — and suddenly she couldn't hold back a smile. Then she turned back to the class:

'Yagodkin! What did I tell you!. . . Vaskin! Watch it, Vaskin!'

I whispered, 'Good morning, Anna Nikolayevna!' And a smile spread over my face too.

'What are you doing? Go away!'

'I told them I had left the iron on at home!'

She almost burst out laughing. It's not a great joke, but she liked it. She liked everything I said, just as I liked everything she said or did.

In the meantime the class was getting louder, with shrieks and thuds, they sensed something. That was dangerous: the door was open, someone could come to see what the noise was about. She turned to the class and put her hand on the door against which I was leaning. Her hand was very close. Small, with thin, sweet fingers, no manicure. In the skin between thumb and index finger there was a blue vein, like a short river on a map, and a white, childlike scar the size of a nail clipping.

'Go away, do you hear me?'

'I'm going, I'm going! I wrote such an explanation for the Nose!'

'Later, later. . . Yagodkin! What is this, really!'

'Do you have five classes today?'

'Four, but I'm staying after.'

She caught my eye and looked at her hand, then back at me and moved her hand away.

'Go, please.'

'I'm going. You won't leave after the fourth period?'

'No, no, I'll be checking homework in the library.'

'Great!'

'Silly!' This is what her look says: this is all nonsense, but I like the way you came here in the middle of the lesson without fear.

Still looking at me, she shut the door.

And I ran back, with long strides, but on tiptoe. I was so happy, so free!

And then we ran into each other each day in the hallways, the cafeteria and library. I hung around the teachers' lounge, I ran to Five A during recess, I caught her wherever I could. Happy, innocent time!

To begin with, after September the first there were several days of torment. She avoided me. I said hello, but she did not respond. I sought her eyes, she looked away. I watched her back, she never turned around.

On the tenth, the Young Communist League committee met, allocating duties for the winter and the entire school year: who would be on the editorial board, who would do mass propaganda, who would be a troop leader for the lower grades. No one wanted that job.

'No discussions!' Pioneer leader Zoya said sternly. 'For the moment we're offering a choice: who wants fourth, who wants fifth, who wants sixth? Otherwise, I'll make the assignments myself!'

'What do you mean?' Voka erupted. 'What if I have no talent for teaching?'

'I did it last year!' Ant shouted. 'Look!' He rolled up his sleeve and he showed teeth marks where some kid had bitten him.

Finally, when Zoya read the list of assignments, I had Five B and Kostya Laskov, also from our class, had Five A.

'Want to swap, Kostya?' I said.

'What for?' Kostya replied. 'I have a brother in there.'

'He has a sister,' Voka joked.

Everyone laughed.

'Let's flip a coin,' I said. I was testing fate. 'Heads.' (I knew it would be heads.)

Kostya took a coin and flipped it.

Everyone waited, even Zoya. 'The coin rolled, jingling and skipping,' as they write in textbooks. We bent down — the coin was heads up.

Later, much, much later, I often said, 'You be quiet, after all I won you with the flip of a coin!' Or she'd say, 'Remember how you won me on a toss?'

Two months later I was the best troop leader in the world. What meetings I ran! What games I invented!

And what were fifth graders? Horrible monsters! Thirty-seven kids! Thirty-seven of them! Like thirty-seven monkeys in one cage! They were incapable of sitting still for two minutes, much less forty-five! Their thoughts were as short as a monkey's and their attention span as long as a bird's. Their energy was like plasma energy: colossal and uncontrollable. Thirty-seven fifth graders, given their heads, could destroy a small civilization in one day.

Think what they do! They drag everything to school: fire, water, earth, trees, metal and mineral, fauna and flora. Animals and birds, dead and alive, gunpowder and tobacco, knives and tools, glass, whistles, slingshots, pictures — everything lying around at home or in the street on the way to school. All day long they squeal, yell, bleat, shoot, spit, cut, saw, spray, gnaw, dig, pick, pull, stuff, burn, twist, untie, glue, unstick. It's not enough to destroy, ruin and spoil. It's not enough to hurt — no, if they pinch, they have to add a twist to it, show off, and watch with vicious faces as the victim writhes and cries. 'Who me? I'm not doing nothing.' They throw their hats at light bulbs, hit each other with book bags and wet rags, they block the door with a chair, stick a cigarette in the skeleton's jaw and tear up each other's bagels at breakfast in the cafeteria. They come to school in the morning looking like normal children and they scoot out at the end of the day as if they had been tortured by demons for five hours.

I think I performed a heroic exploit. I did not spare myself, I put my heart and soul into it. The best way to elicit love is to love. And if you truly do it heart and soul, it's not hard to find ways to do it.

We read, modelled with clay, did target practice, went to museums and movies, ice skated, met war heroes. Their love and devotion were as fierce as their hatred and cruelty. They hung onto me, wouldn't let me walk away. I was the only one who could answer their questions, realize or reject all their ideas.

The kids were in luck: they had an excellent troop leader and a marvellous class monitor. Anna Niko-layevna was deeply interested in the Pioneer work. She sat in the back row during troop meetings and listened patiently, even though she could have left. When we went ice skating, she stood in the snow or sat on a bench wearing a white scarf and white boots, watching and laughing. We would come to an ice-scraping stop in front of her with a flourish and shout, 'An-na-Ni-khai-lov-na-come-to-us!'

She waved her white mittens, and her eyes glowed.

She went to the movies with us, she confessed to never having seen the Egyptian rooms at the Pushkin Museum. When we made a field trip to a printing press, she went with us. She had never seen that, either.

I came up with a simple principle: you can't take *everyone* to the planetarium or zoo.

'Who wants to go to the planetarium? Be honest!'

A forest of hands. Five or six not raised.

'Where do you want to go?'

'The shooting range.'

'All right, next time we'll take whoever wants to go to the shooting gallery. . . Where do you want to go?'

'I don't know.'

'Come on? Think.'

'I don't know.'

'Well, if you don't know, then you'll go with us to

the planetarium, maybe you'll like it.'

Anna Nikolayevna was the most acquiescent of all. She liked going everywhere with us. To the planetarium, to the zoo, to the shooting gallery.

'Take a shot, Anna Nikolayevna!'

'I don't know how.'

'But you want to.'

'I won't be able to do it.'

'Look, you hold the rifle, like that, butt at your shoulder, yes, yes. . . Shut your left eye. The left, the left! ('The left!' came the cries of her students.) See the sight? Look in there. . .'

Our faces were next to each other, her blond hair close to me, peeking out from her woolly hat. I could even smell the lipstick on her lips. I take her unruly hands in mine to show her how to hold the rifle, how to press the trigger. And I see the blue vein.

'Easy, easy, don't worry, see how the barrel is jumping, hold it tighter. Come on!'

A shot! Anna Nikolayevna drops the rifle, the boys laugh, the white target is unscratched. She also laughs and says, 'I've had enough!'

But her eyes are glowing.

In early November, before the holidays, we went to the theater for the first time.

Travelling to the center of town from our neighborhood, especially at night, in a trolley (the number two went to Dzerzhinsky Square) was an event. Broad streets, big buildings, stores, cars. . . Colored lights were burning here and there in preparation for the parade. Men with pulleys blocked the sidewalk, hauling a gigantic portrait up the facade of an enormous building, and powerful klieg lights illuminated it from below. We hurried from Dzerzhinsky Square toward Theater Square, crossing the street at the corner of the Metropole Hotel, and we could see the triumphantly lit Bolshoi Theater, the Moskva Hotel, the Maly Theater and the House of Unions. We were going to the Central Children's Theater. We brought the children across the street. Anna Nikolayevna was in front, I hurried along the stragglers at the rear, the cars waiting and catching us in their headlights. Hurry, hurry!

The theater! The entrance was brightly lit, there were whirlpools around the cloakrooms, some had checked their coats, others hadn't. 'Yagodkin, cut it out, where do you think you are?' Strange prissy girls fluffed up their hair, squashed under hats, and the boys hung around them, pushing and shoving. Why were they separated into different schools? Why had we been separated?

We were in the velvet seats of the front row of the second section. Five A was glowing with clean ears and white collars. They rustled programs, changed seats, dropped coat tags, unscrewed binoculars, and were already throwing things down through the protective netting. There was a roar of voices in the warm hall, a sea of voices. The sounds of instruments tuning up and the sight of the musicians in the orchestra pit tuned you up too, prepared you for something special. We were close to, we were at the very border between life and fairy tale. We were there, and there was the Theater.

Anna Nikolayevna and I were sitting next to each other, she was on my right. She was wearing a dark dress I hadn't seen before with a butterfly brooch. She had a different hairdo, without the bun, and she had changed into high-heeled shoes in the cloakroom. She smelled of perfume. A large purse, which she usually wore with the strap over her shoulder, was on her lap. It didn't really go with her outfit, but I'd never seen Anna Nikolayevna with any other bag. The strap was so long that even though the bag was on her lap, I could play with the strap, twisting it in my fingers.

'It's solid. Want me to bite through it?' I said and bit the strap.

She laughed and pulled it toward her. Her light eyes seemed dark now. The strap smelled of old leather and perfume. I didn't let go.

The third bell rang, the lights dimmed, there was a second of complete darkness, except for the weakly lit orchestra and the red lights with 'EXIT' in blue letters. The final settling down, a stifled yell sounded: it must have been that damned Yagodkin giving someone a last jab.

She was still pulling the strap toward her, and I toward me. My head was pounding deafeningly: boom-boom-boom.

The music played, the curtain parted, and with exaggerated movement actors ran out and spoke in exaggerated voices. A small woman was playing a boy, and the whole audience whispered, 'A lady! A lady!' I saw and heard everything with heightened awareness, but I had trouble comprehending. I pulled the strap and felt that I was pulling her hand closer. Could it be that I would touch her hand? I didn't want anything else in the world. What would happen if I did touch it? I had read Stendhal, I knew what it meant to touch, to take her hand. Incredible. The tension between us grew with every second. But she could simply let go of the strap and not play the game, right? I slowly pulled her hand closer.

On the stage an exceptional boy, but an egotist, has set himself apart from the collective, which is not outstanding in any way, but good. The collective was hurt at first, but then, when the boy left for good and joined up with a bad bunch, it decided to struggle for the boy and save him.

The actors ran around and shouted a lot. There was a lot of wriggling and shuffling in the seats, Five A's attention had wandered. Something was bound to happen. But when they were shown the bad bunch who smoked, played cards, and one not very nice girl even used vulgar language, their attention returned. They stopped laughing.

I made a most daring move, and our fingers touched. We froze. I remembered the blue vein that looked like a short river and the white scar the size of a fingernail clipping. My heart pounded. I waited to see what would happen. She did not move her hand. I touched her fingers. They were like ice. The audience was laughing.

In the intermission we did not say a word and did

not look at each other. She stayed in her seat, I took the kids to the snack bar.

During the second act, it happened again. I held her fingers in my hand. Then I squeezed them gently. And felt a very weak response. It was unthinkable. Happiness.

. . . Snow mixed with rain. Black trees flashed by, street lamps wandered, exploding in ripples over wind-pushed puddles. We were soaked, taking the kids home, our faces cold and wet. Wet snow clung to her shoulders and chest. I took her home, we were practically running. This was the first time we were alone this late, almost the middle of the night, in the empty streets.

Here was the Bird House. We ran into the entrance hall, *her* entrance hall, and shook off the snow and water from our clothes slowly and thoroughly, as if it were the most important thing in the world. We laughed in subdued tones, warmed our hands by pressing them against a radiator as tall as a person. The radiator reluctantly gave off mild warmth. the purse hung by its strap from the valve.

A dull bulb burned. Dark steps led upstairs and down to the basement which reeked of cats. The doors were hung with mismatched mailboxes with residents' names and the names of newspapers. A constellation of bells and buzzers on the jamb, also with names. Many people lived here, but at that hour no one came in or out.

'Go,' she said. She barely looked at me. 'It's late.'

'I'm going, I'm going,' I replied. 'In a minute.'

Our hands were close on the ribs of the rust-red radiator, and I could see the blue vein, but here in the light I didn't dare repeat what happened in the theater. And, probably, I had had enough, I was full as it was. My face must have been glowing, because she looked at me tenderly, condescendingly.

We were silent. A thousand words were in my head, and I felt that if I only dared, I could talk and talk. If only she would say something. But we were silent. We communicated with each other silently. For some reason, we pretended that nothing had happened. What if the weak bulb were to go out then?

She moved away from the radiator with a sigh. A strange sigh. She looked at me from beneath her brows. I was panic-stricken: I had missed something, I hadn't done something. She was waiting. Had I blown it?

'Enough,' she said, 'it's time. Good night.'

'Anna Nikolayevna!'

'Enough, enough, I'm gone.'

'But, Anna Nikolayevna! Another minute!'

'What's a minute? Another minute! It's time!' She stepped on the stairs.

I was chilled by her tone, her words. What had I done? This was a different Anna Nikolayevna. Not the one shooting at targets, laughing at the skating rink, sitting in the back row during troop meetings, giving me her hand in the theater.

I stood, eyes lowered, I didn't know what to do.

'What's the matter? Don't be silly!' she said, as if pitying me. And left.

'Good night!'

I ran down the dark streets, all alone, no more theater, no more happiness, just snow, rain, wind, panicked streetlamps. I had just been happy and suddenly everything changed. Why?

The next day was Sunday, followed by a school holiday. How I suffered! I didn't know what to do with myself. I thought only of her the whole time! How I wanted to see her! How I wanted to go to school!

On the holiday evening, I ran away from my gang and went to the Bird House. I paced on the other side of the street, hiding behind trees, I stared at the bright windows of the third floor. If I could at least see a silhouette! Songs came from the small open windows, men in shirtsleeves and women in dresses ran out into the street. My heart grew cold and fell every time the street door opened. If a woman came out of the distance, I imagined it was she. I got a chill and my feet were wet. I smoked cigarette after cigarette, until there were no more. I didn't see her.

Another day passed. The morning after the long weekend I arrived in school at the crack of dawn. And the first thing I saw was her face, turned to the door. To *me*. The entrance hall was almost empty, three or four mothers were unbundling their sleepy children, an open wet umbrella lay on its side, like a black flower. Neither Chichkin nor the Nose were there, and the technical drawing teacher, Fried Pipette, was reading the timetable with his back to us.

She was sitting on a bench over by the stairs, by a window, huddled in a coat, looking as if she had been sitting there for several days, up all night on duty. She had been waiting for me, she had missed me.

I almost died of happiness. I was ready to throw myself at her feet. How good it felt to see her.

The next second she rose and quickly went upstairs, adjusting the coat which was slipping off her shoulder. I looked around and followed her. On the way I greeted the technical drawing teacher. He looked at me in surprise.

I caught up with her at the door to Five A. She was walking fast.

'Anna Nikolayevna!'

'No, no!' She waved me away without turning around. 'Please!'

And disappeared into the classroom.

I looked around: we were alone, and I went in after her. I shut the door and stopped. A bare light burned in the empty room. She was in the chair at her desk, her face in her hands. The coat had fallen from her shoulders. I didn't know what to do. I didn't know what this was. 'Anna Nik. . .' I wanted to say, but couldn't.

'Oh my God!' she said without moving. And then quickly, turning to me, 'Go away, go away! What's the matter with you, why are you here? Later. . .'

We had time to look at each other, and I thought

that I could come close, take her by the hand, say something.

'Please,' she said in fright, asking me to leave. And I left.

I spent the first period in a daze.

'What's the matter, are you sick?' Voka whispered.

'Get lost!' I replied, seeing only one thing: how she had sat in the empty lobby waiting for me.

What happened after that?. . . I got a note from her. A real note, folded ten times and written on graph paper. She handed it to me herself during the second recess in the cafeteria. The scrawled note said: 'Please come to Kalitnikovsky Square at ten. It's imperative. A.'

I felt that this was a bad note, that it boded ill. I was upset. But that 'A.' at the end, A period, not 'A.N.' or anything else. Then in the note itself there was something school-like, child-like about it that made us equals.

I arrived at Kalitnikovsky Square by ten, to the deserted spot near the cemetery, where you never see anyone in the evening. There was a cold drizzle that created a mush of wet leaves and mud underfoot. She was already there, pacing, holding an umbrella under the one streetlamp not broken by hooligans. The umbrella blocked the light and covered her face.

She began speaking nervously and quickly, almost without looking at me, without preamble. I had to switch to another class's troop. We couldn't see each other. Everything had to be like before when we had merely greeted one another. I had to give her my word that I would do all this.

It killed me.

'It'll be better this way. For both of us,' she said stiffly.

I was silent.

'Do you give me your word?'

'They wouldn't transfer me to another class,' I said meekly.

'I'll ask Zoya about it myself.'

'But . . . it'll seem strange. . .'

'No stranger than it is now. Well, do you promise?'

I was silent.

'I'm asking you. I can't explain it all. . .'

'Of course, if it's necessary,' I said and suddenly asked, 'But what about the kids?' The very thought made me feel hot. Did I *have* to leave them and be next door, in another class? 'I'd rather stop being a Pioneer leader altogether.'

'Well,' she said, still so stern, 'in that case, you won't have to be on our floor at all. . .'

That really hurt. What had I done on *their* floor that was so bad? I was silent.

'You'll understand someday. . .'

There was a groaning sound from the cemetery and a shadow seemed to flicker past.

'Oh!' she said. 'Let's go!'

We went, slipping on the mud and leaves. Water dropped from the visor of my cap and from her umbrella. Near the broken metal of the entrance to the square, she said, 'I'll go first. Goodbye.'

I stopped. Then she vanished, melting in the dark. I was stunned.

But then I realized that she had forgotten to get my word.

She forgot to get my word, and the next Pioneer troop meeting at Five A was supposed to take place in two days. I didn't go to Zoya, and I didn't ask about anything. I didn't go to Five A, I didn't drop in during class, I came late in the morning, and tried to avoid her during the day. Of course, we ran into each other in the cloakroom and the cafeteria and said hello distantly. I saw that she was a bit confused, how could I have submitted so readily?

On the appointed day I went down to Five A. I found myself among a crowd of kids who had surrounded Anna Nikolayevna. They were blocking the corridor.

'Oooh! Aah! Hey!' They surrounded me with squeals and cries and climbed all over me, like Lilliputians on Gulliver.

'Quiet! Quiet! Quiet!' I shouted and hugged them and patted their shaved, ink-stained heads. I looked at Anna Nikolayevna, because she was looking straight at me.

'They won't let me get through,' she said. 'Maybe we should have a meeting today, then? Just one?'

'Yes! Yes! Yes!' Five A shouted.

'Keep it down!' I said. We didn't look at each other anymore. 'Quiet! We'll have the meeting!'

I wanted to show her that I left her alone, but I

wasn't about to abandon the boys, it wasn't their fault.

She sniffed and quickly went back into the classroom. Five A was delirious.

When the meeting began, she sat down in the back row. She took out some exercise books and started correcting them. I saw the bent blond head with the bun at the nape and I was ready to die for that woman.

. . . The embankment, sunset. It grew frosty by evening, and the blurred winter sun sank red over the Kremlin. The Moscow power station steamed like an armored train, black smoke and white steam hung over the entire Zamoskvorechye section. The houses gleamed with red highlights. The sidewalk alternated patches of ice with dry asphalt of a dirty winter color. There was no snow. We had been walking a long time and hadn't run into anyone, but cars sped past us on the road.

We weren't cold, we were warmed by our walking, and we were laughing. Her cheeks were like apples, she swung her handbag on its strap, and kicked a piece of ice along in front of her. I was carrying her string bag containing exercise books wrapped in newspaper.

What did we talk about? What did we laugh at? We didn't even know. We were happy because we were alone together, and the embankment was empty and it was cold and there were puffs of black-red smoke in the sky, and we walked and walked, not knowing where.

Didn't I have female friends who were a bit older than I? For instance, my cousin Valeria or her girlfriend? No big deal! I chatted with them very easily, I joked, and they liked me, I knew that. And I was feeling something similar now, and I spoke easily. At least, I talked and talked. And she listened.

. . . We warmed up in the metro, she had to make a phone call, she was in the phone booth, and I held her purse and mittens. She smiled at me through the glass, looking at me, and her eyes were marvellous.

. . . A fence. A long fence along the Ryazanka. It was about a kilometer and a half long. Solid, stone, dirty-yellow. Beyond it lay the lumber yard. The guards wore floor-length sheepskin coats and they carried rifles. Moscow was still heated not by gas or electricity, but by wood and peat and a cubic meter of logs cost a lot of money.

On the other side of the highway were houses, bus stops, passersby, but here there was no one, and even the buses didn't stop. You could walk along the fence from one end to the other and back and only meet one or two couples and maybe a car going in or out of the one entrance. No one else.

We began meeting there for walks in the evening. And she told me, laughing, that she had first noticed me here, by the fence.

When was that?

During the war the fence became very worn, and the holes were covered with boards. For Moscow's eight-hundredth anniversary, when the city was spruced up, the fence was repaired as well. And it was painted yellow and white, in the colors of the Muscovite Empire. The sidewalk was resurfaced, and along it they planted young lindens, the classic Moscow tree. And here they were, trembling in the cold wind, poor things. Those that had survived and taken root.

We had planted the trees ourselves. The local schools, both boys' and girls', had donated a day's labor. I remembered the day: we were thrilled to be out of class and that a windy spring day was blazing over the city. There were millions of girls in uniform all around, without coats, with bare heads. We talked to them, joked, and laughed like regular people.

With us were our teachers, and the younger female ones worked in a group, with shovels and their hands reddened by the cold, the chilled tree trunks lying in piles on the wet soil. There was a rare sensation of simplicity and equality, because of the amazing youth of the teachers and the excitement of a job done well for our school's prestige. All the others were strangers, but this was our turf. The famous tenth graders were most impressive (they were still in school then), but we mixed with them, joking and laughing. The feeling of accessibility, unity and light-heartedness remained — I can still see people with shovels against the background of that bright yellow fence, the color of a yellow pencil.

I don't know, I must have been doing well for her to notice me. When she spoke, I began to think that I remembered her look, her smile, her uncovered blond hair. But it was so long ago.

Ever since that spring young people used the fence as a hangout. Kids from our school, the vocational schools and the military band school, and the toughs from the Taganka; everyone ended up here in the long light spring evenings. Passions boiled here! Here the acknowledged beauties reigned (with their retinue of homely girlfriends), here notes were dropped and picked up, here the scary Rudik, in a red sweater and his gold front tooth, brought his gang dressed in caps and accordion-pleated boots. Here were gang fights with belts and buckles, here heroes and cowards were born, here kids smoked openly, and the girls came wearing lipstick and thin stockings.

Traces of that stormy and complex life were left on sections of the fence: in chalk, charcoal, brick and paint we wrote what we wanted. 'School 49 is full of jerks!' 'You're curs yourselves!' 'Beat the musicians!' 'I love Vasya' (someone added, 'the fool!'), 'Liza, will be at the movies at 7:30,' 'Zina stinks!' and so on for a whole kilometer.

The interesting thing is that by unspoken agreement, no one ever used four-letter words on that fence.

Then, as it always happens, the in-spot changed to a new place, and only dating couples strolled along the fence. Actually, 'Quadruples,' not couples, because *she* always brought along a girlfriend on the date, and *he* brought a friend. And, as a rule, the girlfriend and friend never stopped talking, while *he* and *she* were silent and exchanged love-glazed looks.

The amount of graffiti went down too. The old stuff faded.

But the third time that I met with Anna Nikolayevna on Ryazanka, I saw a bright, fresh note in chalk: 'Dove! Have a heart! We're at Sanya's.' (My nickname was 'Dove' for some reason.)

I blushed. I didn't want Anna Nikolayevna to see the message. But she did. I had to explain it. Especially since by then she was very worried about our being seen together. And the message naturally meant that the kids knew where to find me.

The point was (very simply) that I was neglecting them. I had broken away. And their jokes and jibes were beginning to represent badly hurt feelings.

Last year we had established a secret 'February Society.' It had started on Captain Stepa's birthday in February, and it was his idea.

Before that we had got along quite happily. We usually met at Sanya Yablochkin's house: his mother and younger brother lived with his father in Germany, while Sanya and his young Aunt Tamara were in charge of the great general's apartments. Tamara, incidentally, had been a pilot in the war and now was finishing up at the Aviation Institute.

The apartment was stuffed with things that were expensive and not Russian. We lounged around like princes on low leather chairs and velvet couches, dragged our wet and worn shoes across luxurious carpets, neither appreciating or noticing them, and drank cheap port wine out of crystal that sang when you barely touched it. We mercilessly pushed on the pedals and tugged at the porcelain pipes of the ancient harmonium, covered with prize medals and enameled tablets with Gothic letters. We roared indecorously, poking our fingers at pink-assed nymphs who smiled over their shoulders at us from gold moldings. We stubbed out cigarettes in an enormous bronze chalice in the shape of a Negress lying on her back with her hands around her knees. Sanya himself despised all this 'rubbish' and sometimes cut up sausage on the top of a unique, encrusted mahogany table, and the slices of home-produced chapped ham and baloney harmonizing beautifully with the pink medieval encrustation.

We were drunk on freedom, cheap wine, and passionate friendship. We shouted songs, wrestled on the carpet and inevitably broke something, either smashing or dropping it. Eventually Tamara would come out from the depths of the big apartment with a towel on her head and command, 'All right, line up!'

Captain Stepa assured us that we couldn't go on like that. We were on a downward slide, historic events were taking place in the country and in the world, and we weren't even thinking about them, much less participating in them. Stepa himself was studying Chinese and planning to devote his life to the unification of the peoples of the Soviet Union, China, and India.

We admitted our guilt: we really were interested in little besides ourselves. But what could we do? Collect scrap metal? Have penpals, like Stepa, among our Chinese friends? Read the papers?. . . We were too late for the war, especially the Civil War, we couldn't work yet, and our Komsomol goal was one thing only: to study.

What else? . .

We were sick of it ourselves, we wanted something extraordinary. We had been brought up on models of heroism, people who had given their lives for their country. But what could we do?

Stepa invented the Society of Februarists. Well, we clutched at that. Even though from the very start we saw that it was just a game, play-acting. Not the Young Guards.

The idea was to master cultural values. Our motto was Chernyshevsky's line that the more educated a man was the more useful he was to his country. We worked out a charter and handmade membership cards. Anyone could join the society if he was interested in any field of science, technology, literature or the arts, and could teach the others something they didn't know. The proposals flowed in: nuclear physics, the history of Napoleon, graphology, Chinese painting, 'What is poetry?'. But Zheka Borisov proposed 'The Development of Turtles.'

Stepa was offended.

'Listen,' he told fat Zheka, 'we're talking about things that interest man most in life.'

Zheka nodded amiably: he understood.

'Are you really interested most in the development of turtles? What turtles? Why?'

'Why not?' Zheka said. 'Just imagine if there were no turtles.'

'And why can't he lecture on turtles?' Sanya said in his defense. 'Don't pressure him, Captain. Everyone chooses what he wants.'

'What the hell do I care about his damned turtles!' shouted Stepa. 'You're mocking the idea! For the sake of Mother Russia and turtles!'

'You never know,' Sanya said mysteriously.

All this had happened the year before: the society was created, three or four lectures were given, but then came spring, exams, and there was no time for graphology and turtles. We were going to start seriously in the autumn.

And here was the winter and I had missed one meeting, then another, and a third.

I told Anna Nikolayevna about it. In order to calm her down, I told her with irony and sarcasm, laughing, thinking that she would have a laugh, too. But she didn't.

She looked at her watch and said that I could still make the meeting. I shouldn't neglect them because of her. And then she asked anxiously if anyone knew about our society. I was surprised.

'No,' I replied. 'It's secret.'

'That's the problem! You'll have to stop it immediately, this isn't a game!'

'What's the problem?'

'You're acting like children! Do you know what happened at one school?' She named the number. 'The children there also came up with some secret society, they published a newsletter. . .'

'So?'

'So? They mocked everyone, the director included, and . . . and some of the kids were simply. . . You must stop this, I'm telling you seriously. No membership cards or program, for the love of God!'

She was agitated. I couldn't understand why.

I didn't go to the meeting, of course, we walked, even though on the way back the message — 'Dove! Have a heart!' — struck my eyes painfully. And I promised both Anna Nikolayevna and myself that I wouldn't neglect them any more.

But then strange days caught me up in their whirlwind. We said one thing and planned to do another, reasoned rationally, then did a completely different thing.

Two days later we met for the first time in broad daylight — in another part of town, in another neighborhood — and went to the movies. To a matinee, in a strange theater.

That was strange all right! I traveled alone on the trolley and the metro while she — strange! — went the same way, to the same place, also alone. And I was to stand outside the movie theater in the middle of the day, while she came around the corner, passing behind the thick, winter-bare bushes. I could see only her head, the brown woolly cap, her face — a strange, urban, common face, because she had not yet noticed me. I had already bought the tickets and was holding the blue paper in my hand. My hand was in my pocket and I didn't have exercise books or textbooks and neither did she, not even her big bag — as if we weren't really a student and a teacher.

Barely a third of the theater was full. It was an old place and cold, and I was sure that we were being watched by the usherettes, two little old ladies and a man of twenty or so with a bandaged eye. We had a whole row to ourselves and waited for the dim lights to go out.

And while we went in, waited in the lobby, then found our seats and sat down — she kept talking rather loudly and animatedly, as if for the sake of the others, about how much she had wanted to see this film, how good it was that we were going to see it, how she had never been able to find time to see it before. Even I started to believe her. We had seen almost half the film, without understanding a thing, before I had the courage to take her hand. Strange.

And then we had a trip to Kotuar, also strange.

Sunday morning at seven o'clock. It was still and dark, the Kiev Station was lit up as if at night. We got onto the train, and I just couldn't believe that I was with this group: Anna Nikolayevna; Lubov Petrovna; Lubov Petrovna's friend, Gleb, a tall and skinny pilot; my pal Sanya Yablochkin together with his Aunt Tamara! And also Petr Antonych, Lubov's father, a youngish, animated man in a long top coat and a hat with ear flaps, the kind children wear.

It turned out that Tamara and Lubov Petrovna had known each other a long time (through Gleb). Lubov Petrovna's parents lived outside town, in Kotuar, where they had their own house with a garden. The forest was nearby, and there was lots of snow. They had already been there, made the trip, and had a marvelous time. You could relax, ski. And it was all so simple! Lubov Petrovna invited her girl friend Anna Nikolayevna, then Gleb and Tamara, and Tamara suggested taking her nephew, Sanya, and Sanya invited me. Very simple. It turned out that Gleb and Tamara knew Anna Nikolayevna too, they were part of the same crowd. And that morning at Kiev Station it occurred to me for the first time that besides the school and Five A, besides me and her memories of the killed Orest Chestnokov, 'my' Anna Nikolayevna had and should have another life, unknown to me. What a thought!

Lubov Petrovna was in charge of the trip. I was embarrassed and I sensed that Anna Nikolayevna was too. For instance, I had never been a particular friend of Sanya's and, to tell the truth, it was strange for him to invite me. I had accepted but didn't mention it to anyone else. Why hadn't I at least invited Voka, my best friend, to join me?

Unlike me, Sanya behaved with calm maturity: he laughed at the jokes, told some himself, called the pilot Gleb and called Petr Antonych 'Gramps'.

So, there we were. Bags, packages, Tamara's and Sanya's skis, Petr Antonych had two new zinc buckets (everyone kept asking him where he got them) and the buckets were full of stuff too. As far as I could tell, we had food and drink and even some records.

Anna Nikolayevna was wearing a white fur jacket and a white knit dress. The outfit was very becoming and without high heels, in felt boots, she was tiny, half a head shorter than I.

We were traveling on the commuter train, on old bits of rolling-stock with small cars. It was unexpectedly crowded, and we couldn't get seats together. The skis had to be kept on the observation platform at the end of the car, and eventually we all ended up in that cramped area. Only Petr Antonych stayed in the car — he'd run into fellow Kotuarians. It was cold on the observation platform and smoky, there were strangers, grim folk, apparently night-shift workers. Our merry group seemed out of place. I kept expecting someone to come up and ask me, 'And how did you worm your way into here, pal?'

Lubov Petrovna kept us amused, she was like a fish in water here. But even that embarrassed me: seeing a teacher acting simple and merry, flirting with a pilot, a cigarette between her teeth. She was telling a story.

'During the war I spent two years on this train delivering milk to the city. My father will tell you. I went down to meet the first train at five in the morning. I delivered to apartments, I had steady customers. Had to climb up to the sixth or seventh floor. And as soon as I sold it all, I'd leave the cans at the last apartment 'til evening and hurry off to college. I was never late once!'

She laughed, Gleb hugged her, playing with her shoulder, and said, 'So that's why you're so round, milkmaid!'

Sanya cleverly came back with a story of how he was forced to drink milk as a child and how he used to pour it into the flowerpots. Tamara told of a cow that lived at the air field in their squadron. I could have told them how that summer in the country I drank a two-litre mug of milk in one go, but I didn't have the nerve.

That's how we traveled, and soon we arrived. We piled out cheerily and walked a long way single file down a path through the snow. Lubov pushed her Gleb into a snowbank. The wintery day was only just beginning, the lacy white forest stood in the distance, chimneys smoked evenly over snow-covered rooftops, dogs ran around, and red magpies with long tails flew from fence to fence.

We came to a clean, warm house, where we were met by Lubov's mother, young and plump, more like Lubov's sister than mother. The house smelled of milk, and we were shown the cow in the shed. We took off our shoes and walked on the warm floorboards in our stockinged feet. Seeing Anna Nikolayevna without shoes, in such a homey fashion, was so new to me that my heart almost stopped.

Then we had breakfast and went outside. Sanya and Tamara went cross-country skiing, while Lubov pestered the village kids to let her use a sled. It was a steep run, the sleds flew down to the edge of the railroad tracks, and a train was traveling along, with people looking out the window, adults like us, while we sledded. Among us was a man in uniform, his long legs stretched out, on a kid's sled.

Anna Nikolayevna was afraid at first, but Lubov forced her onto the sled, gave her a shove, and Anna Nikolayevna whizzed down to the bottom, laughing.

Lubov and I jumped onto a noisy metal sheet with its front curved up and hurtled down after her with a howl and a squeal.

And down there. . . we, the two boys, overturned the sled, together with the dog Damka that had been pestering us since morning, we, the sled and the metal sheet — all tumbled into a snowy pile. Anna Nikolayevna was flat on her back, arms flung out, gasping and dying of laughter, snow on her face and her hair, her scarf had fallen off. I was on all fours, my hands sinking in the snow, my hatless head pressing against her chest, and I was snorting like a dog. Lubov had ended up with her head in a snowbank, sweeping a boy along with her. Damka was leaping and barking joyously, the kids on the hill were shouting and hollering, and Gleb laughed and clapped his hands.

Her face, her lips — there they were. Our cold cheeks touched. I had to lean on her shoulder to pull my hand out of the snow. Laughter, screams, everything was possible. It would have been so simple, so natural to kiss her! Wasn't she lying there too long, unprotected, relaxed, as if waiting to see what would happen?

But I didn't dare. How could I? Who was I and who was she? And in public too. We were too close as it was, suspiciously close. And even though the whole day was leading up to something, had been given to us by fate and was taking us somewhere, I still didn't believe it, didn't succumb.

Then we had lunch, and drank, and Petr Antonych offered us roast rabbit, and I felt strange again. How could we all be sitting at one table, clinking heavy glasses? Sanya and I were given less to drink than the others, but Sanya just laughed. He liked to tell of his amazing adventures: quite a series of them. (We could never check since they always took place in Germany when he was visiting his father.)

We were having a good time at the table, everyone with reddened faces, when suddenly Lubov began teasing me, with hints about Anna Nikolayevna.

'Lubov! Really!' Anna Nikolayevna said and blushed.

I thought I would die on the spot, but the group seemed not to have noticed. Everyone was talking, everyone had his own topic and seemed to forget about what had been said. Two seconds later Lubov was talking about something else.

But after that, we were afraid to look at each other.

Lubov, Gleb, and Petr Antonych of course, were sleeping over at Kotuar and planned to take the early train to work the next day. Tamara, on the contrary, was in a hurry and shook Sanya, who had fallen asleep on a trunk. Anna Nikolayevna asked me several times if my mother knew where I was and would she worry. She brought that up frequently. Naturally, I waved off the question. I think we could have stayed, things were going that way.

But I could see that her mood was spoiled, she wasn't laughing at Lubov's jokes and, like Tamara, she was in a hurry to leave.

It was completely dark when Lubov and Gleb walked us back to the train station. I was embarrassed to look at them, I knew why they were staying. We traveled in a crowded train and had to stand in the passageway. More and more people got on at every stop. Tamara was pushed into the car, Sanya was shoved face against the window of the second door, which didn't open. We ended up shoulder to shoulder in the crush, backs against the wall, and there were more backs in front of us, smelling of cold air, old, poor clothing and suburban roads. To stay together, I took Anna Nikolayevna's hand. I did not let go, quietly caressing the nail-shaped scar, as we rode and rode — a trip that was strangely fast and strangely long. . .

Her entrance hall once again. Dull light, doors with mailboxes. She was backing up the stairs, facing me, as I advanced on her from below. She held on to the bannister with her left hand, and with her right she poked a finger at my forehead.

'Go away! Go away! Go away!'

She laughed. I continued my advance and looked up at her, a happy slave.

'Go away, I said! Go away, didn't you hear me?'

Today she was wearing a coat with a gray collar and a gray rabbit fur hat with ear flaps, which made her look young and wild. A girl and a boy. She kept saying 'Go away!' and I shook my head: no, no, no.

We got up to the second floor, I continued pushing her on.

'Not another step!'

She laughed, but I advanced. If she were to stop, we would be face to face on the same step.

There were two flights of stairs between the second and third floors. There was a small landing. A narrow window was cut in the wall: you had to lean out in order to see the street. The window was protected by three heavy metal bars. You could sit down to rest on the top one, and it shone, polished, reflecting the street lamp outside.

She plonked herself down, tricking me. Not another step! And she was happy to have tricked me. How could I advance now?

Ah, so that was it! I sat down next to her.

'Go away, we won't both fit!'

'Yes, we will!'

Our legs blocked the window, nothing was visible, no lights burning above or below. We sat, as if on a perch, resting our feet on the bar below.

'Stupid old fool!' she said to herself.

In response I quickly found her hands. I knew them like my own by now. I pressed them and barely kept my balance.

'Please, oh, please!' she whispered right over my head, her lips almost touching my hair: I had pulled off my hat downstairs. I didn't listen to her. I kissed her hand where the scar was, her fingers.

'Oh, my God!' Her sigh was bitter and weary. 'What is this?'

'Anna Nikolayevna,' I whispered with all the tenderness I could muster, 'Anna Nikolayevna, oh, Anna Nikolayevna! Don't. . .'

As if to console her, I caressed her shoulder, my face touching the perfumed collar. I caressed the collar, everything was floating before my eyes. I'd forgotten where I was.

I touched her cheek with my hand, very lightly, hardly at all. And suddenly she responded, pressing her cheek against my hand. God, I'd never felt anything like that. There was so much tenderness, trust and loneliness in that gesture. I swear to God, I was ready to cry, I understood her so well!

And that went on a long time, I wanted to do it over and over again. The amazing proximity, it was so good, so good, so quiet. . .

We were frozen, even though my fingers were caressing her hair, were tangled in her hair. And obeying my movement, her head went back slightly. Now our cheeks touched. Now we pressed our foreheads together, like children playing a butting game. My hand was on the back of her neck, and suddenly her hand touched my head and squeezed my shoulder. My heart thumped and her lips were close to mine. . .

Then I was walking in drizzling rain, the snow melting, slush underfoot, the empty streets filled with fog. I was trembling with joy. I sniffed my fingers, which smelled of her hands, her hair. The scent of lipstick floated around my lips in the damp air. I walked not knowing where, unable to go home, my face bursting with a smile.

Over and over I gave her that one and only, long, clumsy and joyous kiss, the first of my life, funny, uncontinued, unrepeated, heart-breaking.

I circled and circled the crooked lanes, cutting through the connecting inner courtyards. The city was deserted. I was alone with myself. Two policemen on white horses rose out of the fog. Their hoofbeats rang on the street. The horses were white, the men in black jackets, blending into the darkness, and it felt as if the horses were on their own, without riders.

'Hey! Come'ere! What are you doing out so late?'

'I'm going home, sir, home!' I shouted from afar and slipped into the first courtyard. I didn't want to talk to them.

Over and over I touched her cheek, tangled her hair, felt her head bending docilely. I played that record a hundred times and put it on again.

Then I came out on a familiar street — Khiva, the 'Hussar's', the white house. Everyone was asleep, no one knew. The steambath loomed black, no lights on, the gates shut. The door of the beer hall was fastened with a padlock the size of a beer mug. The white house slept a doll's sleep. In the park, water dripped and splashed from the black poplars, their crowns dissolved in the mist.

The school seemed to have vanished. If I hadn't known its contours by heart, I would have seen nothing but blackness and fog ahead. The porch light wasn't even on.

I stopped. My brain was in a whirl: September the first, Five A, Margosha, Voka, Chichkin, the Nose, Anna Nikolayevna. I felt I should bow to the school, get down on my knees before that porch: thank you, school! But now, suddenly, I felt anxiety, something nasty and mean emanating from that black building. Like the scary bedtime story: 'In a dark, dark city, on a dark, dark street, in a dark, dark house, in a dark, dark room, stood a dark, dark coffin. . .'

The dark, dark school was threatening me: what are you so happy about? Think what you two are doing! Think, think!

I heard hoofbeats behind me, and in the distance white horses' heads the size of chess figures floated into the lamplight. I didn't wait for them to come closer. I ran home.

The Nose called me in.

His office was on the third floor, in a cramped, windowless room. It used to be a storeroom but had been turned into the room for military science: wooden rifles were kept on trestles here, and we used to march with them. There were two real rifles and a submachine gun, and we took them apart and put them back together again under the supervision of Vasya, the military director. Homeless Vasya, back from the front, used to live illegally in that room before the Nose came. The room still retained Vasya's smell: damp overcoat, leather boots, shag tobacco, the alcohol fumes that emanated from Vasya in the mornings, and burnt wheat gruel, made from unmilled grains cooked for hours on the electric hotplate in the corner.

It was about two years since Vasya had left the school, the place had been painted and repaired, and the Nose had put up glass-fronted book shelves filled with various collected works probably of Soviet 'classics' like Stalin and Marx and his beloved files with their tied up ribbons. The walls were covered with portraits and a political world map; and Ivan Ivanovich himself sat at the big clean desk with a lamp. But as soon as you walked in, you smelled Vasya, I swear! You looked around, could it all be gone? No old overcoat hanging on a nail, no hotplate in the corner, black with burnt gruel? The coils were always burning out and Vasya twisted them into knots where they broke off, and the knots heated more than the rest of the coils, and made sparks, and soon the whole contraption would burn out again.

I should have expected to be called in by the Nose long before now: I'd never had so many D's.

'What have you got to say for yourself?' the Nose asked. 'How am I to understand this?'

He sat at the desk, I stood head bowed. The desk lamp and the milky overhead light were on, as if it were evening, when actually there was frosty sunshine outside. Our class register, covered with green paper, lay before the assistant principal.

With nicotine-stained finger and his nose (almost) bending low over the book (today his nose had a sticking plaster X on the right side), the assistant principal followed the line next to my name. He'd come across yet another D and say, 'Well! Another one!. . . Look here, the second semester is ending, it's half-term, and look here, you've got: D, D, C, C, D! What am I supposed to think?'

'I'll fix my grades, Ivan Ivanovich. . .'

He didn't listen. 'And this D, D! Eh? Skipped three classes. We skip classes, too, do we?. . . Another D!'

'Where? Where?' I moved forward. 'I didn't have that D! Where did it come from? I'd like to know!' I was ready to haggle over an illegal D I had forgotten. 'I'll clear this up with her, really! What else!'

'Look here, cut it out!' The Nose stopped me short. 'You're wasting your time on all sorts of nonsense!' He looked straight at me. 'How many times have you been told about your hair? You're all walking around like monks with long hair! Why haven't you gotten it cut?'

'I believe I'm no longer a first grader. . .'

'Drop it. Look here, it doesn't matter if you're in first grade or not, you're still in school! Your head is filled with the wrong ideas.'

So. It wasn't just my D's. He had another bone to pick with me. Had he smelled something? No wonder Anna Nikolayevna feared him so much.

The assistant principal flicked aside the register and leaned back. He took out half a cut cigarette from a metal box, put it in a stained cigarette holder and lit it. I would have loved a smoke then, myself.

'You have clothes, shoes, all the best,' the Nose was saying. 'You've got it too good. . . What's going on with your Pioneer work?'

There it was! Steady!

'. . . Look here, I hear that you're in the fifth grade night and day! In school till after dark, off on all kinds of excursions!'. . .

Well, come on, what else do you know?

'. . . with your grades' — his hand indicated the roll book — 'you'll have to cut out all these extracurricular activities, all of them! And get a hair cut, that's final! Look here, a person has to be getting A in everything: clothing, his head, both in body and mind!'

No, you old Nose, you don't know everything! I had to counterattack in order to protect her and to save myself.

'Your first priority is your grades! And what are you thinking of instead?'

'What do you mean? What am I thinking of?'

'That's what I'm asking you. Look here, what have you been thinking of?. . . We are going to free you of that Pioneer work, don't worry about that. . .'

My heart sank.

'. . . and then we'll see what other reasons. . .'

'What does the Pioneer work have to do with it? I'm quitting school!'

I don't know why I said it. I realized that he didn't know anything for sure, but he must have heard rumors. And I had to lead the Nose away from that right now, get him started on something else. All that 'We'll free you,' and 'We'll see,' implied not only the person speaking but a council, a collective. Or Chichkin's office where they might have already talked and decided my fate.

The Nose fell for it, he grew wary. They didn't like losing seniors.

I maintained my silence. I stared down at the raspberry-colored runner on the floor. The Nose took two drags on his cigarette.

'How am I supposed to take that?'

I waved my hand airily, as if to imply there was too much to tell. 'I'll probably have to leave right after the New Year. . .'

And I paused mysteriously again. I could smell Vasya in the room and remembered him. I missed him.

'May I be excused, Ivan Ivanovich?'

My expression implied that if I started talking I'd burst into tears.

'Wait, now look here. . . What? How?. . . We weren't informed. . .'

'I have to go to work.' I looked up at the white ceiling, then quickly back at the Nose. I hung my head again. 'My mother . . . in bed all winter . . . she'll be getting invalid benefits. . .'

I was astonished by the nonsense I was making up. But I couldn't stop. 'Her legs . . . barely walks. . . And my little sister too. . . Fourteen. . . TB. . .'

My mother worked like an ox, with two jobs, and my sister was a gymnast at a children's sports school. That could be checked in less than an hour, but I lied anyway. Superstitiously I thought that my mother might truly get sick from what I had said and that my sister would develop TB, but I went on lying. My counterattack had to flatten the enemy so that he couldn't even lift his head.

The Nose drummed his fingers on the desk. He believed me and yet didn't believe me. I had to make him fall for it completely.

'We don't have enough for medicine. . . It's all on my shoulders. . . And we're all in one room. . .'

'What about your father?' he began and then remembered. 'Oh, yes, of course.'

'Five days before V-Day.'

I heaved my deepest sigh and if he had expressed the slightest doubt I would have let him have it about my father. Even frontline soldiers would have gasped at my vocabulary! (My father was missing in action back near Kursk, and I knew absolutely nothing about his war record.) I decided to finish him off.

'Why do I hang around school? Because I don't want to go home, it's like a hospital there. I get a little distraction here. With those fifth graders. . .'

The Nose wanted to speak, but I didn't let him. 'I feel bad about it. But I'll have to leave.'

'But, look here, this is all news to me!' The Nose got up and paced around his desk.

I remembered the time we tossed some cartridges into Vasya's porridge and waited to see if they would explode.

The Nose muttered, 'People don't know, but they say. . .'

'What?'

'Nothing, I was just thinking aloud. . . Yes, yes. . . Well, if you have to work, you have to, but, look here, it's a shame. You're in the ninth grade!'

'I'll go to evening classes, with the vocational guys.'

The assistant principal made a face: they didn't like night school either. If it happened which was very rare that a student from night school transferred to day school, he was put back a year.

'My own son finished night school, when I was in the army. He never got into any college after that. . . Oh dear, you're basically a gifted student!'

He looked at me as if bidding me farewell. I was beginning to believe my own story, I felt as if I was leaving tomorrow. I looked at him with regret.

We were silent. I think I could have sat back then, crossed my legs and ask the Nose for a smoke.

Then the assistant principal realized where we were, said that they couldn't let me transfer with my D's and, despite everything, I had to shape up.

'I will, I will!' I said casually. 'I just need a week with the books. . .'

'Fine! Now look, you're a gifted student!' He repeated it. 'We'll give it some thought, we'll talk about it . . . off you go now!'

I even felt sorry for poor old Nose by then. I was ashamed. I lingered in his doorway. But the assistant principal was back at his desk, scribbling in his diary — probably a note to check on my mother — and his crepuscular office was severe and cold again. It still smelled of Vasya. I left.

People know everything instantly in school. In the sunny corridor, where I was squinting as if I had just come out of an X-ray chamber, Voka was waiting for me. I laughed.

'Well?' he demanded.

'Nothing! My grades. I gave him a story though.'

I was proud of myself. I figured I'd confess to my mother and ask her to at least say that she was sick or had been sick. She'd rescue me. I would have to do some studying, bring my grades up by the end of the semester. I was ashamed of myself really. And it would be better for Anna Nikolayevna and me: less attention. It's one thing when a top student breaks a window and another when he's a trouble maker.

I calmed down. I even did some studying that day. But in the evening it all went downhill.

That evening Anna Nikolayevna and I met on Kalitnikovsky. Strangely enough, the horrible Kalitnikovsky park became our refuge. No one would ever see us there. Of course, there was a cold snap, but that didn't bother us. We would go to the very last bench in the back, where no one ever walked by.

Anna Nikolayevna was in a panic. I had laughed, bragging about how I had tricked the Nose, but she wouldn't even listen to that. She made me repeat our conversation over and over in all the details.

'I knew it, I knew it,' she muttered. 'It was bound to happen. . .'

I tried to console her, I said that the Nose didn't know anything for sure. He must have heard an off-hand comment, no more, otherwise he would have used a different tone with me.

'No, no,' she replied, 'I just feel it . . . it's in the air

. . . if not today, then tomorrow. . . We can't meet anymore, do you understand? We have to break it all off. I know it will end horribly if we don't. . .'

'Calm down,' I said. 'Relax. Don't be silly.'

'No, you don't understand! You don't!'

'All right, all right, we'll do as you say. . . I'll leave school for real. Want me to?'

'Because of me? Are you crazy? I'm ruining things for you as it is!. . . I'm a horrible, horrible woman. . . Feel your hands! You'll catch cold. What am I doing?. . .'

A minute later we were embracing like mad. As if the whole school would come running, the Nose in the lead, to pull us apart forever. What was happening *between us* was more important than the Nose, stronger than fear.

. . . Cold, cold, the icy bench, snow up to the seat, and we had swept snow from the bench. Far in the distance a lone street lamp, under which she had waited for me with an umbrella, but here it is dark, just reflections from the snow: when your eyes got used to the darkness, there was enough light from the snow to see faces.

Right behind us was the cemetery fence: brick posts and iron bars. Further back the church window glimmered with reddish votive lights. The church itself had dissolved in the dark and the lights seemed suspended in midair. The tips of the cast-iron spears of the fence were topped with snow cones. There were close rows of snow-mounded graves, heavy epaulets of snow on the crosses, the rustle of dry wreaths — yet I sensed someone was out there, silent and staring.

It was around eight o'clock, no more, but it seemed as if the night had been going on for a long, long time. Time had stopped, sounds had vanished. Once in a while, from Konnaya Square, came the jingle jangle of the trolley through the icy air, a reminder that somewhere there was a city, tracks, human life.

My left hand lay in the sleeve of her sheepskin jacket as if in a muff. It was warm in there, while the right hand, around her shoulders, was stiff in its flannel glove and could barely move. She took my hand between hers and rubbed and blew on it, then put it at the base of her throat, pulling the collar over it.

I stopped moving, losing all sense of what was happening to me.

'No!' She shook her head, rubbing against the bench, her hair coming undone, her scarf falling off. 'No! No! No!'

'Anya! Anya! What's the matter?'

I was bewildered. I didn't know what to do. I tried to pull my hand away. She held tight. I wanted to kiss away her tears. She recoiled sharply. But a second later she put her hands around my neck with a force I didn't expect from her and whispered, *no, no, no, no. . .*

And suddenly she let go, pulled away, pushed me like a sled that was supposed to go downhill on its own.

'It's awful,' she said. 'It's all so awful.'

With trembling hands I lit a cigarette. We avoided each other's eyes. She hurriedly fixed her hair and re-tied her scarf. In the time it took me to cup the match in my hands to avoid attracting attention in the dark, she had pulled herself together.

What had just happened? What was happening? Why were things so complicated and unhappy? It was like being under a scourge. Ever since that time in Kalitnikovsky it was hard for me to look at her, to talk to her. I needed time to be myself again. The hatch to our underground privacy shut slowly. For the time being I couldn't tell us apart. I wanted to pinch myself: is it me? I thought so.

We left. She picked up some snow in her mitten and pressed it to her lips. She walked a bit ahead of me. I could barely move. I was wearing my father's boots, which my mother finally gave me that autumn. She had been saving them, and they had been too big before, anyway. The boots were of fine leather and quite chic, but as cold as ice.

There was the street lamp and there was the entrance. We went past it and dissolved into the darkness again. No one was around, not even a dog, but we had to part there. She adhered strictly to this rule.

The house numbers glowed dimly; raspberry lamp shades still shone in windows (what time could it have been?). The two-storey Old Believers' fortresses stood hostile and huddled together: stone foundation, wooden top, solid fences, yawning doorways.

'Do you understand that we cannot meet anymore, ever?'

I sighed. I had heard this every night.

'God, why didn't you fall in love with some school girl? You could date her without being afraid. . .'

I laughed.

'Really! Don't torment me! You can see I can't take it anymore. . . It's stronger than me. . . I don't understand anything. . . You must help me! Don't come, all right? You should be doing your homework, catching up. . . Are you listening to me? Why aren't you saying anything?'

'I won you. . .'

'This isn't a joking matter!'

'I'm not afraid of anything.'

'That's what you think. But I'm afraid of everything. There can't be anything between us. Do you understand? Never!'

'But why, why?'

She did not reply. She sighed.

'Anya!'

'What, what? What?. . . My darling, my silly, what?. . . You don't even know.'

We threw ourselves at each other again, a kiss, another kiss, our cheeks frozen, even our lips. I held her as tight as I could, she yielded to my arms, we were both out of breath.

'Don't come tomorrow! Please try! I can't go on this way!'

'Oh, Anya, Anya! Just tomorrow, one more time. And then I promise. . .'

'You won't come? For sure? After that you won't come?'

'I promise. . .'

We were almost weeping, believing what we were saying. Even though we had said the same thing yesterday and the day before.

The trolley bell rang, scaring and separating us.

'That's all! Until tomorrow! Don't follow me!' She kissed me quickly and ran ahead. I stayed behind, like a runner thrown off by a false start.

There was the intersection, there was the light. I could see the white boots and white coat flick past. From that second I started waiting and wanting only one thing: to see her again.

I hesitated a bit. The cold attacked me like a dog. Could it be that cold? My ears, feet, hands, and nose all felt it. Should I wait for the trolley? If I did, then I could pass her, jump out at the turn, where she'll be going onto Maly Khivinsky, and with a smile, casually, bow and say, 'Good evening, Anna Nikolayevna!'

I would have done that before. But now it was not a joking matter. And we couldn't be seen together. Why didn't we worry about being seen before?

Damn it, it was so sad! I never prepared myself for saying good-bye, and the isolation overwhelmed me. Why couldn't I see her home? We were turning into hypocrites like everyone else, we lied like the rest. We could kiss but we couldn't walk home together.

I wouldn't have gone anywhere, I would have sat and waited at the stop. But the cold forced me to move. There was no sign of the trolley.

I ran out onto Ryazanka. Ground snow blew across the broad highway as if across a field. The street lamps swayed. There were few cars and no pedestrians at all. On the other side was our fence: endless, in both directions, as far as you could see. Deserted.

At home everyone was warm, asleep or going to bed. No one cared about us. Flowered night gowns, creaking bed springs, women fluffing up pillows, old women braiding their hair, men rubbing one foot against the other before putting them under the sheets, a young woman covering a yawn with her hand, a warm shoulder with a strap, a young man stuffing an open book under his pillow and getting comfortable on his side. Light switches: one light out here, one there. . . I could smell the herring and cabbage stink of our poor building, could see the dim, spiderweb-covered lights in the hallway with its six separate doors. I'd be home soon. I'd lie down carefully in the dark in my cold concave cot, and my mother would mumble a sleepy question and fall dead asleep. I could go to the smelly kitchen to do my homework or read *Jean Christophe*. . . I couldn't be alone anymore! Everything had changed, everything had lost its meaning. I didn't want anything. How could I go and lie down in that cot with all these feelings inside me? How could I sit in that smelly kitchen? How could you live if you'd become a giant and had to return to a matchbox?

I ran across the highway, in the path of a truck.

The harsh headlights met my eyes. If I were to stop, he wouldn't be able to brake in time. . . Strange, I hadn't had thoughts like that before. . .

I ran along the fence. I couldn't warm up my feet. I held my nose in one hand and rubbed my ears with the other. All I needed now was frostbite. I didn't want to go home.

'Dove! Have a heart! We're at Sanya's.'

Oh, my god, I couldn't remember the last time I had seen the guys outside school. I was suddenly aware that they barely talked to me at all now, never asked me anything, and that I didn't ask them anything either, and when I did, I didn't listen to the answers.

Should I drop in on Voka? Too late. His father would answer the door and say, 'You idiot! What are you doing running around at night? Is the day too short for you?'

What about Sanya? I could sleep on his warm couch, amid pink nymphs with melon breasts, under the chandelier with bronze cupids?. . . It would be nice, but my mother would be crazy in the morning, worried about me.

I didn't know how I ended up at the Ptichkin house. Her two windows were still lit. She must have just come in. I couldn't stay out on the street anymore. I ran into the building. I put my hands on the radiator. I pressed myself against it. It was tepid. But still warm.

She was just upstairs, so near. Should I run up the stairs, knock, ask her to come out? Not go in, ask her to come out. Why couldn't I do that? Let her be with me just a little bit longer. I couldn't remain alone.

Not allowed.

I didn't know why, but I knew it wasn't allowed.

I smoked. My hands shook. I thought I would burst into tears.

I sat down on the dirty cold step and sat, hunched up, for a half hour or more. Shaking.

When I left, her windows were still lit. She wasn't asleep. Don't sleep, please. Be with me. . .!

I was sitting in class, writing to her. Outside, it was gray, just like the day before and the day before that. Fast snowfall, black branches and wires whipping around. The class was quiet: either napping or listening to Margosha blathering about the noble literature of the nineteenth century. Voka was reading a novel under his desk.

I was writing a long and complicated letter, I couldn't express clearly on paper what had become so clear in my mind the past few days.

We hadn't seen each other for several days. Not on Ryazanka, not on Kalitnikovsky, nor on the embankment. Just in passing at school. Her mother had pneumonia. 'It's a punishment, a punishment!' she said. She ran around getting medicine and sat at her mother's bedside for hours at a time. I sensed that it was better to lie low. Not even come near. I lay low.

I discovered tons of time: I learned physics, did experiments with Voka, went to the movies with him. I spent one evening at home with my mother and little sister, and my mother said, 'What an honor!'

She minded her own business, I took care of mine. And in just two days, I got back into it. We were catching our breath.

We had planned to meet Saturday night, just for a half-hour, but something happened. And Sunday too. There was no way of getting in touch on Sunday, neither of us had a phone. Then that terrifying moment came: no plans were made for meeting, the thread was cut, and I didn't know anything about her or she about me. A centrifugal force had grabbed us and carried us apart.

Sunday morning, Mother and I went to the Petrovsky Market to buy me a pair of felt boots and then dropped in on Aunt Raya, Mother's sister. The whole day gone. We spent two hours at the market in a huge crowd. The whole city was there. We got separated and then found each other. There were a lot of boots for sale, but I didn't want second-hand ones, and new ones were too expensive. I didn't want felt boots at all, but my mother insisted. She compared prices, haggling wildly, maneuvering through the crowd, her face flushed, her hair peeking out from under her scarf. Men kept trying to pick her up, and she told them off. People swarmed, the snow was churned into mush underfoot, militiamen blew their whistles, crooks sneaked around. The sellers stood in meandering rows, each a one-man store, at his feet all kinds of things spread out on a sack or newspaper: shoes, dishes, primus stoves; on one shoulder a coat, trousers or a dress tossed over the other, more clothing on outstretched arms, and on top of the scarf or hat were two or three hats and caps. They stood like urban scarecrows from morning till night.

'Your son?' they would ask about me.

Mother would reply, 'he's mine, of course he's mine!'

Then she would push me forward a bit, look me up and down, pat me on the shoulder. She liked showing me off. I would look at my feet. The old women clicked their tongues and complimented my mother: she was so young, hard to believe she had a son this big.

'I'm not young!' she would reply. 'Just not used up!'

In the open air, in daylight, Mother's flushed face really was young and pretty, eyes sparkling, slightly colored lips playing in a smile. She laughed and her beautiful teeth shone. What a marvel! I had seen her every day but never like this, I didn't even know that she had blue, iridescent eyes, though they were in deep shadows.

Finally, as often happens, we ended up buying completely different things than we had come for. Warm socks and an old gray sweater for me, a skirt for work for my mother and tights for my sister.

At the flea market they also sold cooked food and traded vodka for bread, bread for sugar, sugar for canned goods. We bought hot pies filled with offal, and then, feeling generous, Mother gave me three kopeks for an ice cream. I gave her some as we walked and her teeth, as white as the ice cream, took bites at it as she laughed.

Merry, carrying packages, we showed up at our relatives' house, not far from the market, three stops. The gray morning was still lingering. It had been a long time since I had last seen Aunt Raya, her husband Uncle Volodya, and my cousins, Valeria and Anya; a long time since I had climbed the porch steps of the old, long, one-story house, familiar to me since childhood.

They were glad to see us, everyone was home. Valeria was still asleep after working her night shift. She lay on the couch with her face to the wall, her hair spread out on the pillow. Anya was ironing by the window, and Aunt Raya was getting her husband ready for the bath house. Anya grew embarrassed and ran out, she was wearing a short robe that was too tight and torn under one arm. I was astonished by her rounded body, the bare woman's legs and arms: she had been a little girl only yesterday it seemed, and now, just look!

Incidentally, we all looked alike: Mother, Aunt Raya, Anya, Valeria, and I. I remember reading somewhere: 'We all came from the snub-nosed, shy peasantry.' And I thought of my relatives, as if it had been written about us.

Uncle Volodya was a completely different type. He could have come from an icon. Long-faced, thin, dark-eyed, with an old expression of dissatisfaction and quiet suffering. He was taciturn. He would sit and say nothing. Smoke and cough. When he was ready to say something, he'd start coughing. He'd wave through his coughing fit — as if to say, the hell with you, why did I ever start? — and cough instead of speaking. He had come back limping from the war. He worked as a driver on a heavy goods truck and went on long hauls.

I felt guilty. Uncle Volodya loved me and I had forgotten that he existed. He said hello huffily. I asked if I could go to the baths with him.

We went. We stood in line for an hour and a half and got cold and when we finally reached the warmth and water, spent another hour and half washing and steaming. Uncle Volodya slapped his skinny body with birch twigs until it shone. His left hip and thigh down to the knee was disfigured by a horrible blue scar: as if a shark had bitten out a chunk of meat.

I suffered while he steamed and soaped. I almost howled while he rubbed my back, and died while he sat and sat in the dressing room, getting his breath, sweating, his eyes shut like an old bird's.

While we waited outside I had been amused by the talk around me. In the baths I watched the chatty, tipsy towel man in a white robe lecturing his customers, and the tattooed fellow who had pictures even on his calves: a parachute on one leg and a mermaid on the other. Many of the men, like Uncle Volodya, bore traces of the war on their bodies: scars and blue gunpowder burns. Many were with their sons. Looking at the children, I remembered how I used to go to the baths before the war with my father. He would put me in a small tub of water and spin me around. . . He'd put some hot water in the tub, put it on its side, pour in some soap, and whip it up with a back scrubber until it was all foamy. He'd put me down on a bench and lather me up. I remember giggling and squealing like a pig because I was delighted and ticklish. Then he'd take me across the slippery floor to the showers and put me in under such a strong spray that I had trouble breathing. I used to squeal, laugh, and jump.

'Remember, Uncle Volodya, how we'd go to the baths with Father?' I asked.

He began to reply, but he had just lit up, still naked in his bath sheet, and instead of answering, began coughing and waving his arms at me: how could he not remember! And then coughed for about two minutes.

Lunch was waiting for us when we got back home, and the women scolded us: where had we been? But I think they liked waiting for us, they were glad the men were back from the baths and they could feed and take care of us.

We didn't hurry through lunch, the way everyone did then, but ate a Sunday meal, family style, almost as if out visiting. A long meal, with zakuski, herring and pickled mushrooms — some had fish soup, others had cabbage soup. The women drank grandmother's homemade cranberry brandy, Uncle Volodya and I had pink vodka, made with elderberries, two glasses each.

The kids sat on the couch — the severe Anya and Valeria, untalkative like her father, and me. Our mothers laughed at us, at how much we resembled each other. Anya and I pointed at them and said, you look like each other, too. My mother was even more flushed and merry. She and Aunt Raya were recalling their poor childhood, and even though there wasn't anything good about it, they remembered the happy and funny times. They laughed and we laughed with them.

It was getting dark outside, we turned on the lights, but stayed at the table, drinking tea and talking. Anya told me about her school, I told her about mine, but only the funny things.

Then came a young man in a hat, long coat, white silk scarf, and gloves. Aunt Raya bustled about, called him to join us at the table, but he did not remove his hat and gloves and stayed in the doorway. Valeria got up and made her way across our feet — seven marble elephants fell on Anya and me from the shelf over the couch.

Valeria went out into the hallway with the young man and Aunt Raya and Anya, whispering and interrupting, explained that he was Valeria's fiancé who kept calling, and worked in the Criminal Investigation Department or something like that, and had a room in the middle of town, but Valeria kept brushing him off and didn't want to marry him.

'She's right! She shouldn't!' Uncle Volodya said suddenly.

'No one asked you!' Aunt Raya said. 'Quiet!'

'Oh, God!' my mother sighed.

Valeria came back in and asked Anya and me if we wanted to go to the movies. We jumped up.

We went. It was very crowded, but the young man — whose name was Andrei — got in another way and quickly came back with tickets. The film was exciting, an American one about cowboys and Indians. Anya cried out or shut her eyes during the scary parts and grabbed my hand. At the end she wept.

'Anya! Anya!' I said consoling her and suddenly was amazed: it was only then I realized that Anya had the same name as Anna Nikolayevna. I had been saying the name all day long without connecting it with Anna Nikolayevna. It was as if it were an empty sound. And I hadn't thought of her at all for several hours. Where was she? How was she? Why was I sitting here with another Anya?

We went back. Valeria and the mysterious Andrei went for a walk. Mother was tired of waiting for me. She was bored and yawning. Uncle Volodya was asleep on the couch, Aunt Raya was sewing; they had cleared the table and washed everything up.

Mother and I had a long ride home in a half-empty trolley. She napped with her head on my shoulder. She'd jerk up at the stops: is it ours? I wanted her to rest and kept saying, 'Sleep, sleep.'

I ran to school the next morning, afraid. Of what, I didn't know. Our meeting. Nothing was clear. How was she? It felt as if something had happened. She had got over me, without me around. I'd run up and find the teacher Anna Nikolayevna, a grown up.

Blond hair, severely done in a bun, which made her look much older. 'I must ask you to use the formal mode of address with me. . .' Was that possible? Why not?. . . I was so afraid that I slowed down, I didn't run, I dragged my feet. It was almost a relief to see that Five A was already out of the entrance hall. The bell was ringing.

We wrote compositions, we had a double period with no break. Then Captain Stepa detained me and said that I was being summoned to a meeting of the Society of Februarists.

'Summoned? What do you mean? What for?'

'For everything,' Stepa replied. And wouldn't explain.

The feeling grew that something I didn't know about had happened.

I was in third period feeling time go by. One minute, another minute, a third. I had to act, find out, *know*, and I was just sitting there. What was happening on the second floor? In the teachers' room? In the Nose's office? What about Anna Niko-layevna? What the hell was I wasting time for? Another minute gone. And another. And another.

I looked out of the window, and on the second floor she was looking out too. We were looking at the same poplar, snow, and street. How was she looking? How did she feel? Why was I so afraid? I couldn't stand not knowing. But perhaps that was better.

Nonsense! She was waiting for me. She didn't know where I was. She was going crazy. She was exhausted by her mother's illness, she was tired, she needed help, and I, like a pig, had abandoned her. Every passing minute stabbed her in the heart. Hurry!

The bell rang and I rushed out of the room. Hurry! Hurry! If she doesn't see me at this break, she'll die. Hurry. I rushed down one staircase, another, jumped down the last four steps and . . . bumped into Chichkin. Right into his stomach.

It's amazing I didn't knock him down. The impact threw his glasses from his nose, he lunged for them, caught them (thank God!), put them on and, hands still raised, made fists and shouted, 'No running!'

'Oh, Ivan Mikhailovich! Excuse me, Ivan Mikhailovich. I'm sorry, Ivan Mikh. . .'

'Hold it! Don't move! What's your name?. . . Oh, so it's you!. . . Silence! Up against the wall!'

This was taking place on the landing of the second floor. He grabbed me hard by the shoulders, and practically shoved me toward the wall by the window, beneath the marble board with the golden names of the tenth-grade group.

'What? Why? Answer!'

I glanced sideways in the direction of the corridor and saw my Pioneers, waving their schoolbags, coming out of Five A and lining up. Were they being let out? After third period? Why? Where was Anna Nikolayevna?

'Answer me!' Chichkin shouted and jabbed me in the shoulder with his sturdy, sharp finger.

Five A's eyebrows shot up.

Then I felt Anna Nikolayevna come out.

'Excuse me . . . it was an accident. . . I was on the way to the library . . . it's urgent. . .'

'If — Everyone — Runs!. . .'

I knew they were looking at me. I tried to stand more casually.

'Attention!' the principal yelled.

Poor Anya! She didn't even know what was the matter, that he was howling over a trifle. She would think it's about her. But I couldn't look at her or let her know. Poor Five A! Their leader, their idol, was being tortured before their eyes.

'I'll show you the library!. . . You'll stay after school!'

'Ivan Mikhailovich, I. . .'

'Silence! Attention! You'll stand here! All break! Don't move!'

He jabbed me one more time painfully, nailing me to the wall, then turned sharply on his heels and went toward the corridor. Kids were pouring out of every door, swirling, like water out of sluices. The principal cupped his hands around his mouth and shouted 'No running!' so loud that the little ones froze, as if the principal were playing 'Statues' with them.

Marching like a wind-up toy, Chichkin headed for the stairs.

I shrugged, laughed crookedly and tried to look relaxed. I saw Anna Nikolayevna's pale face, almost in a faint, and the frightened, compassionate eyes of Five A. Now they were pouring out of the classroom and their line came close to me. Anna Nikolayevna was in her everyday blue knit dress, her hair particularly smooth, the bun particularly tight (a sign of a very bad mood), with a tired, exhausted face. She had a briefcase and exercise books in her hands. Suddenly she leaned against the door weakly, stood for a second, then went back into the room. I didn't have time to give her a signal to console her.

The principal's voice was roaring upstairs. I couldn't leave my place, and the children didn't dare come any closer to me. We had to stand where we had been placed. Between us was the landing and part of the corridor.

The corridor was boiling, filled with kids. The teachers moved among the close-cropped heads as though fording a waist-deep river. Half a minute later other kids were picking on Five A out of envy for their early dismissal. There were snotty remarks, jabs, someone kicked somebody else's briefcase. They buzzed around me too, like bees, pointing at me, sticking out their tongues. Five A sensed that there would be a delay in going home, and they were worried.

When Anna Nikolayevna reappeared in the doorway, the line was gone. In its place, a noisy snake of school children rattled. Yagodkin was at its tail, spitting across three people at a fourth kid. The head of the snake was a huddle of kids, arms and legs sticking out of its jaws.

I moved forward, I wanted to show that it was a trifle, I smiled guiltily. She did not respond and looked past me.

'Yagodkin!' she shouted angrily and jerked him by

the collar. She didn't know how to shout, it didn't become her, and she grimaced whenever she raised her voice.

'Yagodkin!' someone squeaked in imitation.

'All of you, back in line immediately! Now!'

I felt it again: time passing. Passing, passing. Not minutes, but seconds ticking away. If I didn't do something immediately to break up this awkwardness between us, to return to *our* life with a look, a smile or a word, if I didn't break through to her, I would remain a boy in the corner while the teacher, Anna Nikolayevna, a grown woman, would lead her class away without a thought for me. I don't think this had ever happened before. What was this?

She moved forward to the head of the line, to lead the class. I tried to catch her eye, but she turned her back on me, facing the kids. They moved. Now only the landing was between us.

I winked at the kids: don't worry, this can happen to anyone, see I get into trouble like you. They didn't know how to respond, their smiles were grim. Besides which, they were afraid that I would hold them up, too.

I took another step forward. The head of the line was level with the stairs.

'Anna Nikolayevna!'

She looked up. She could have been looking at me for the first time in her life.

'Are you leaving? Are you letting them go?' (As if I couldn't see that she was leaving and letting them go.)

She nodded quickly, a miserable, pathetic woman, and stepped onto the staircase. Was she afraid? Or did she not want to talk to me?

I took another step. She gave me a frightened look: are you crazy? Don't! I stopped. At least, that was live and real.

Chichkin, like a god from above, roared. I stepped back.

At that second, Anna Nikolayevna started downstairs, and her blond head with the metallic bun vanished. I leaned against the wall, resting the back of my head on the lower edge of the marble board. Boys ran all around me. The white door of Five A was open.

'What's going on?' I wondered. 'An adult, tired, *strange* woman. Pathetic. Her mother is sick, she's exhausted.' I was trying to find excuses for her, but I knew it wasn't her mother. 'She's exhausted in general. And whose fault is that? Mine. Isn't she insisting, begging that we end it? And am I helping her? I think only of myself: to see her, to catch her, to touch her, to kiss her. But what about her?'

I was ashamed. I wasn't thinking of Anna Nikolayevna and me the way I usually did, not about myself, but only about Anna Nikolayevna alone. Damn it! I should have looked at this a long time ago: she was an adult, smart, serious. Then there was me, with my childish face and shabby coat with my arms sticking out. Just think: she ran to meet me, I kissed her in dark corners and on benches! It must have been so hard for her, so shameful! It cost her so much! And I was insulted, I demanded, got annoyed, angry even. I was so ashamed! Remember how they looked at us when we went to the movies? Remember how they looked at us in the train when we went to Kotuar? Oh, my God! What could I do?

I understood! I would write a letter. Everything would be different now. She had to know that she had nothing to be afraid of. I would fix everything, clean it up, change it. She would not have to suffer on my account.

It was so clear what had to be done that I couldn't stand still. The break wasn't over, but I left, not scared of Chichkin's wrath. I was writing my letter.

I wrote it during one class, then another. I wrote it when I got home, I wrote it all evening — I knew we wouldn't meet again that day — and now, the next morning, I was writing again. I had a hundred plans to expiate my guilt, to save her peace of mind. I would release her, I would leave if necessary, transfer to another school, join a military academy. I would never again demand anything from her or allow myself anything until I grew up and became independent. So that she would not be ashamed of me and have to hide me from people. Yes, yes, she would be able to look people in the eye and not blush. I swore to that.

I was thankful that we had realized this in time! Now she could say to anyone she feared — be it the Nose or her mother, whom she mentions so frequently — she could say, 'Nothing happened.' Her conscience was clear and had to be clear.

I wrote my letter, tore it up, started again. I believed myself, and it never occurred to me that I was afraid of losing her, afraid of her sobering up. I was prepared to do anything so I would not have to watch her look through me.

Another class passed. I didn't have the nerve to go downstairs. When the letter was ready, I would go to her bravely, hand it to her, and from that moment on everything would start anew.

In technical drawing class, where people did whatever they wanted while Fried Pipette drafted a projection of a screw or something in solitary enthusiasm on the board, I finished the letter. Voka continued reading, but now the book was placed openly on his desk. He knew what I was doing and must have expected to be given the letter to read. But even though Voka knew almost everything, I had been letting him in on my affairs less and less of late. Voka couldn't understand everything. I think that he didn't believe me, that he suspected that I was keeping the most important thing from him. That I was protecting a lady's honor. It would have been silly to try to dissuade him.

'Well?' Voka asked, looking at me as if I were sick.

I did not reply. I folded the three pages with writing on both sides and put them in my pocket. Voka guffawed. Then he said, 'You don't remove the army if you want to capture the fortress.'

'A lot you know!' I said. 'Why don't you deliver this instead?'

'Now?'

'Yes.'

Really, I thought, now. Voka will give it to her and that's that. I took out the letter and gave it to him.

Voka got up and left without saying a word.

'Where are you going?' the technical drawing teacher asked meekly.

'I'll be right back,' Voka said.

'You should have asked at least,' he countered.

The class buzzed in anticipation of an amusing scene.

'There he goes!' Ant bellowed.

Fried Pipette tucked his head into his shoulders.

'Excuse me,' Voka said, 'I'll be right back.'

The teacher waved him away.

Mentally I accompanied Voka as he went down the hall, the stairs, along the corridor to the door of Five A and opened it. There she was. He handed it to her with a smile. She was surprised. Maybe she blushed. Voka ran back. Corridor, stairs, corridor. There. He should be coming in now. . .

The door opened and Voka came in. He sat down, catching his breath. He nodded to me: everything was fine. I looked around. The class was observing us. Me. Had they guessed? Probably. But it didn't matter now.

. . . First there was the church. We entered, and inside was a cemetery, crosses coming out of the floor, stone ones, taller than a man, the cross bars like outflung arms. We walked and walked, a narrow slit of light ahead, a passageway. Further on, it was divided by a barrier made of stand-up pipes, like the entrance to a stadium, so we had to separate, let go of each other's hands, but we couldn't do that at any cost, and we went on even closer together, like a bride and groom. And it wasn't Anna Nikolayevna, but a girl called Tanya, rather it was Anna Nikolayevna and Tanya. Her name was Tanya, that's for sure. We decided to go that way and I knew that the stadium barrier went right into my hip and into her hip too. How could that be? But there was no blood, no broken bones, thank God. We got off easily. It turned out that this is Kotuar, but now it wasn't winter, it was summer, dark blue clouds all across the sky, and a strange boy ran up and asked if we'd seen his model airplane with a real engine. He had set it off and now he couldn't find where it landed, though it was around here. Where? I wanted to look too, but Tanya suddenly unbuttoned her dress over her chest, and it wasn't a dress but a white kerchief and she wasn't wearing anything underneath. I could see her naked hips and belly. Was she crazy? People were looking. Of course, there's Petr Antonych, Lubov Petrovna's father, he was leading a cow and chuckling and shaking his head: well, you kids are really something, naked in broad daylight! But she wasn't afraid, she was laughing, and green young rye, such a bright green, was all around us, its ears still soft and silky, an endless field of rye under summer clouds, but the rye was only knee high, how was she planning to hide in here? The boy was running around looking for his plane. It was embarrassing. But she went on and on, her back to me, I saw her naked and I was afraid, I knew that I had been tricked, she was a stranger. She was a nymph from the painting at Sanya's house, she wanted to lure me somewhere. Why was I following her? What a fool, I should have been running away. And then this lizard appeared, with glasses on its protuberant eyes, tiny human hands, and a cigarette burning in its fingers. Only it wasn't a lizard, it was our neighbor Osorukova, who was only pretending to be a lizard, because she knew about Anna Nikolayevna and me. But she was prepared to help us. She wouldn't tell anyone. I ran through the green rye, it was getting thicker, it was hard to walk, but Tanya called to me and I came. She was lying in the rye, arms over her head, naked — blinding. Between her arms and between her legs the rye pushed through in bundles. She didn't fall down and flatten the rye, she's been lying here waiting for me so long that the rye grew around her, outlining her. And on her stomach was the beautiful, red-and-chrome plane, the model plane the boy was looking for. Tanya laughed: look where it landed. She wanted me to take the plane away, she wanted me to come close. I was stunned, I knew I was being tricked, that people were lying in wait to mock and shame us. I thought I saw Yagodkin's face. The Nose was here somewhere, and also the British diplomat Michael Darnley, into whom Captain Stepa had turned. They were all hiding in the rye, that was for sure. I approached fearfully, because I was certain that Voka's girlfriend Natasha had taken on the image of Tanya and Anna Nikolayevna. It was her, but I couldn't do anything about it, I came closer, I bent down. The plane was gone. That was a trick too. I suddenly realized that this was just a nightmare, that I had to wake up immediately and then I would be saved, but I couldn't wake up. . .

What are you supposed to do after a dream like that?. . . It doesn't melt when you wake up, it doesn't vanish. It sticks in your memory. All morning I was as quiet as a mouse and distracted. I could still picture the green rye, the lizard woman, the plane and the rest. It caused more confusion than shame in me. Could it be true? Do other people have dreams like that? Either they don't remember or don't want to tell. Was I losing my mind? After all, I had decided on just the opposite!. . . And how could I look Anna Nikolayevna in the eye after a dream like that?

And then I got a note! Voka brought it. My heart began thumping and my knees grew weak. The paper was rolled into a tight tube the size of a match stick.

So many things came into my head. I was afraid to open it. I even imagined that Anna Nikolayevna knew about my dream. I worried about a brief, insulting word. I forgot that this could simply be a response to my letter.

How relieved I was, how happy, when I opened it. It said: 'We must talk.' Three words. Calm, radiant words! I heard her voice, her tone, I saw her face. We must talk. But of course! How simple! Of course, we had to talk! We must talk! Absolutely! How good! The hell with the days, with this loneliness. That meant we would see each other. We'll see each other, we'll talk, I'll tell you everything. How much I missed you! We must talk. There's so much I have to tell you. Thank you. We must talk. We must talk!. . .

During break I rushed around school looking for her. I couldn't find her.

'Have you seen Anna Nikolayevna? Hey, guys, have you seen Anna Nikolayevna?'

We bumped into each other on the stairs. She was going down, I was going up. We froze for a second, staring into each other's eyes. What a look. Her eyes were smiling with a touch of mockery.

'Hello, Anna Nikolayevna.'

'Hello.'

She was holding the bannister with her left hand, I held it with my right. Sturdy blocks of wood were glued to the railing and painted the same color: the Nose's invention to keep us from sliding down it.

Smiles, smiles, forty-five smiles in a minute and a half! And the stairs! We were just the way we had been that evening, when she retreated upstairs and poked me in the forehead with her finger. Pupils flowed around us. Raisa Yakovlevna's voice came from upstairs.

'When?' I asked.

'At ten. In my courtyard. I can't leave the house until then. At the back entrance.'

'Got it. . . How is your mother feeling, Anna Nikolayevna?'

'Better, thank you. We finally got her fever down.'

'Thank God.'

'Yes.' She kept trying to move on.

Raisa Yakovlevna, surrounded by little boys, appeared above her. I made way. We separated.

At ten! At ten! Wonderful! Today! In her yard!. . . I couldn't keep from smiling. I said hello to Raisa Yakovlevna on the run. She peered at me too closely. But I wasn't afraid of her. At ten! Ten! Where was their back entrance?

That day I did my physics exam, got an A from Margosha in literature and a B in geography. And I managed to tell Anna Nikolayevna about it: I ran into her in the cloakroom after school.

Then I hurried home and studied hard until evening. Everything was going well, and I kept repeating, 'We must talk, we must talk. . .'

Exactly at ten I entered the yard of the Ptichkin house. Strange, I had never looked in there. The yard was enclosed on the right and left by a wooden fence, and straight ahead, deep inside, stood a two-storey cabin with three or four windows lit up, weakly illuminating the snow and the dark path. In the middle of the yard was an old tree with spreading branches, like an oak. It was very quiet and the only sounds were the distant rattles of the trolley from the street.

There were several lights on in the main house as well, including upstairs. Two back stairs came out into the yard, two doorways under rusted metal awnings. I figured out that I needed the left-hand entrance. I headed for it, sinking in the snow.

Didn't anybody ever walk here?

I pictured earlier times, before we were even alive, when horses were driven into the yard, servants ran up and down the stairs with samovars, carried wood for the stoves and baskets from the marketplace. Maybe wandering pilgrims sat under that tree and they were brought a pot of yesterday's soup through the back entrance.

I wasn't afraid of being seen or meeting anyone. I was trembling with anticipation. The back entrance gaped at me, a mysterious hole. Its doors must have been torn off a long time ago. I was expecting a white figure to appear in that black hole. This didn't seem like the best place for a talk, there wasn't even a bench, but all right, she knew better. Even if she came down for just a minute, I wouldn't hold her up now.

Near the entrance a heavy wrought iron gate leaned against the wall. Who had torn it off and why? As I came in, I had seen its mate, still dangling in place. The snow looked beautiful on the iron curlicues. There were steps going down, they were also piled with garbage that was dusted with snow. How would she get through here?

Suddenly I heard snow crunching and quickly stepped back into the shadow: a man was walking toward the cabin from the gate. I didn't understand what was the matter with him at first. He was swaying and he was carrying an upturned chair on his head. The man was muttering to himself. I heard: 'So, cast a stone at me! Cast a stone at me!'

He took a long time walking to the cabin, and I was afraid that Anna Nikolayevna would come down just then and be frightened by him. The man bumped the chair around the porch, swore, and then there was silence.

I looked up: a shadow had blocked the window and then the small window pane opened on the third floor. A hand came out and waved upward: as if to say, come upstairs. And waved again: the way people wave when they can't see at whom they're waving but are sure that there's someone there waiting. My heart thumped, the old way, the way it had at our other meetings.

I didn't walk down the steps, I jumped holding onto the broken gate, stepping bravely into the dark. It stank of cats, cellars and garbage. I struck a match. Snow covered pipes underfoot, balconies of the same wrought iron design as the gate with broken railings, a large pot on its side with a rusted, kicked-in bottom. I had to go carefully here. . .

I moved cautiously, like a cat, circling rotten

furniture, the headboards of rusty beds, old painters' stepladders and iron barrels filled with refuse. I kept seeing the white hand beckoning me.

I was very quiet near the doors: there were noises in some apartments — water flushing, voices, radios. Again people were living a normal, peaceful life, while I was creeping behind their backs like a thief, on their back stairs, listening like a spy to things I shouldn't hear. At any second a door could be flung open, light would burst over me, and there would be ten faces, ten pointing fingers from the doorway, ten cries of 'Gotcha!'

At last I tiptoed across the third-floor landing and stopped by the door. Silence. Dark, cold, silence. Even in that cold the door smelled of the kitchen and old things. With my fingertips, I could feel the old oilcloth that upholstered the door. I had figured out that all the doors that opened onto the back stairs led to the kitchen. And there were always dozens of people in these overcrowded kitchens, cooking, washing, gossiping, warming up. How would she come out?

I listened. It was very quiet. She wouldn't have signalled me from the kitchen if someone had been there. Hold on. Calm down. She was simply waiting. I could feel her on the other side of the door, quiet, tense, waiting for a signal. I knocked ever so gently. And jumped back.

Instantly the old door came unstuck, opened with the toothless smack of an old woman's lips, and in the narrow crack I saw gray laundry on the line, a sooty wall, kitchen shelves filled with glass jars, and felt a gust of warm, fetid air. I narrowed my eyes, like an animal in a moment of danger that thinks if it can't see, then it can't be seen.

A second later the door was shut with a creak and something warm and soft, homey and sweet smelling, familiar and new, like an awakened baby that you lift from its bed, fell into my arms.

'Anya!'

'Quiet!'

'Anya!'

'Quiet, my dear! My silly, be quiet!'

We couldn't have had a better talk! Hugging, kissing, whispering each other's names, laughing and weeping with tenderness and joy. Everything was behind us, all the torment and fear! There was no passion yet, no electricity in our touch, and we had enough breath to whisper, talk, and laugh. She was like a balloon filled with light in my arms.

Suddenly we did begin talking, talking avidly. About my letter, about every day that had passed, about pharmacies and medicine, about the long Sunday, about the nurse that came to give her mother injections, about Voka and physics. We had to clear up everything, put back everything that had been lost during those days. We were choked with laughter, remembering how I had slammed into Chichkin's belly. We didn't leave out a thing, we discussed it all.

'You're not cold?'

'No, no.'

She had her coat over her shoulders, and underneath a light house dress with short sleeves. Her arms and throat were bare, and I could see that her elbows were bare when she pulled the coat closer.

We talked about my letter. I repeated that I was prepared to do whatever was necessary, to leave whenever she said.

'I read it and thought: maybe you really do . . . love me.'

'How can you say that, Anya? Of course I do!' I pressed her elbows.

'And if . . . if you do, then maybe it's even worse.'

I didn't understand, but I agreed: 'Yes! Of course!'

'No, it can't really be love. . .'

'Why, why do you say that, Anya?'

'I don't know.'

'Damn it. That again! You just said. . .'

'Quiet, quiet! Just listen to you! Swearing!'

Really, I didn't want to go back to that old, dark torment. I forced myself not to speak. I quietened down and let go of her. I sought a change of conversation.

'Well, well,' she said. 'What's the matter?' Then whispered, 'Why don't you give me a hug? I have to go.'

I wanted to ask why. I stepped back, ready to leave without even a handshake. 'You have to go, but we haven't settled anything,' I wanted to say.

Suddenly she spoke, casually, almost by the way. 'Why, why do I have to give this up? I have nothing

. . . nothing except you now. . .'

I didn't know what to say, I was taken aback.

'Well!' she said with determination and embraced me.

And froze: someone was moving in the kitchen.

Her lips slid across mine quickly and then she pushed me away: 'Run, darling!'

Like thunder came the voice that could have belonged to the old door itself: 'Why the hell is our back door open? With the bolt thrown back?'

I jumped away, Anna Nikolayevna opened the door, letting the light burst out. She had a bucket in her hand, she must have prepared it ahead of time, and with the words, 'It's me, Ivanovna, me!' she vanished.

The dark blinded me. The emptiness exploded like a bomb. I had just had her in my arms. I could hear voices behind the door, but I was cut off from the world, in prison.

I didn't know that the Nose and Margosha had gone to a meeting of our society that very evening and that Voka's mother and father had found his diary which had everything about Anna Nikolayevna and me in it.

. . . Voka and I were at 'the Hussars,' sipping

warmed-up beer and clearing the air. No we weren't. He said nothing and neither did I. The windows in the beer hall were covered with hoar frost, the place was empty and smelled sour and damp. Nura with the mustache coughed and cursed each wracking cough. The lame old woman who washed dishes gathered up the mugs, giggling to herself, tipsy since morning. We were there instead of school, instead of being in class. We stood at the bar, doomed souls who didn't give a damn, getting miserably drunk. To hell with the damned school! Voka was smoking, finishing his third mug, and not looking at me. Lousy scribbler! Conspirator! He hadn't even told me that he had a diary. And if he did have one, why didn't he go ahead and write about himself? Why bring other people and things you know nothing about into it? And the stupid jokes, like I hope our Dove doesn't make a pass at Margosha! And details about Anna Nikolayevna. Some joke!

'Shooting isn't good enough for you, you idiot!'

He just looked out the window you couldn't see through and said, 'You think I didn't catch it, too?'

'Serves you right!'

The idiot naturally wrote everything about his Natasha and — even more shameful — about this Marusya, who did housework for them and whom he felt up whenever he could. When his mother and father read that, they collapsed on the floor next to the desk where they found his diary.

His father simply smacked him on the face with the diary: 'Take that, Maupassant! I'll show you

Marusya! And take this for Natasha!' But his mother, a real pain, convinced that her little boy had fallen into a bad crowd, put the diary into her bag and went off to school. She wept in Chichkin's office, showing him pages of the notebook: read that, see what's going on in your own school!

It was amazing how Chichkin reacted: first of all, he said he didn't believe it and trusted his teachers, secondly, he never read other people's diaries, even children's, and didn't intend to start now and he had no respect for people who did.

The mother started threatening to go higher, to the city authorities and so on. But the Nose showed up, took a sniff, figured it out, calmed her down, took her to his office, heard her out, promised to look into it and kept the diary.

After that Voka threatened to hit his mother with an iron, had a hysterical fit, left the house, burst in on the Nose, demanded his diary and shouted so loud that people came running. The Nose had to fend him off with a chair. In other words, he created a real scene. And naturally the rumors at school started. Who? What? Why?

. . . We're outside the Nose's office, Sanya, Captain Stepa, Zheka, Ant and I, hissing at one another, arguing. I want to go with them, but they say that since I wasn't there, there's no need to go asking for trouble, no one knows what will happen to that lousy society. Of course, the Nose came to the meeting when Zheka finally got to give his report on the development of turtles, but that just confused him even more: what kind of society was this, and what did it have to do with turtles?

'What's the matter with you?' I say. 'Who do you take me for?'

And Captain Stepa replies condescendingly, 'What are you getting so excited about? You basically left the society. . .'

I look at the guys, but they stare at the floor and say nothing. Sanya shrugs.

'Well, I'll go on my own, I'll tell him!' I say.

I'm saying that, but to tell the truth I'm almost glad that I'm out of this problem at least. I've got enough on my plate. And I think, being really lowdown, that if they get grabbed by the gills, then I'll confess, too, but if not, why look for trouble, really?

Margosha rolls along, hurrying down the corridor. Everyone looks even grimmer and turns away. She has learned about our society a long time ago and we have confided in her, she has even been to a meeting (without me, though). But to bring the Nose!

She justified it by saying that the Nose had called her in and interrogated her: there's a rumor, he said, that your students are meeting secretly, reading reports. She explained as best she could. 'Why do they meet outside school? And why isn't it supervised by the Komsomol organization?'

'They're all Komsomol members, it's probably

more interesting for them this way.'

'What does "more interesting" mean? Do you know what you can get for secret societies?'

'Why don't you go and hear for yourself?'

'I will, I'll get to the bottom of it. There aren't going to be any secrets at our school!'

So Margosha said that she was trying to protect the society and free it from all suspicion. 'Thank you, of course,' Stepa said reasonably. 'But what kind of a secret society is it where the Nose sits in? Sorry, I meant Ivan Ivanovich.'

'Don't say that!' Margosha clucked. 'Don't even mention the word "secret"! It's not secret in the least!'

'Not any more, it isn't,' Stepa said.

Margosha reaches us and stares at me: she knows that I must be a part of the society. But Sanya took a step forward and blocked her view of me. I said nothing.

'Well, shall we go? Come on,' Margosha babbles. She is frightened herself. 'Don't worry, nothing to be afraid of. Ivan Ivanovich is merely going to legalize everything, so as not to let word of this dangerous "secret society" out where there could be serious trouble.'

To keep it all inside the school walls.

And they leave: Captain Stepa, Sanya, Ant, Zheka, and Voka. And I remain behind.

. . . After his conversation with Voka's mother, our

principal Chichkin called in Anna Nikolayevna without any diplomatic niceties and asked, 'What about
these rumors? Are they true or not?'

She muttered, 'No,' but her face was red, and she
couldn't look up at him. She barely made it out of his
office.

The next day the Nose called her in, and she
handed in her resignation.

Then the Nose called me in.

But I haven't reached that part yet. First I had to
talk with her. . . . Voka and I were sleeping on
Sanya's green velvet couch. We had smoked and
drunk Malaga, and he was asleep, while I stared at
the light from the street lamp shimmering on the
ceiling and the chandelier. What should I do?. . . I
wasn't going back home, I wasn't going back to
school. My friends were gone, she was gone. I had
nothing. Nothing and no one. I was gone, because I
was a traitor and a coward, helpless, and any plan I
came up with was no good. My only thought was
this: I go into the Nose's office and spit in his face. I
have a taxi waiting outside, I take Anna Nikolayevna
by the arm. We leave the school in front of everybody, get in, and drive off. Where? Where?. . .
Damned stupid youth, empty pockets, worn shoes.
Remember how they looked at you in the train: what
are you doing with her, kid?. . . But whom did we
bother? Whom did we hurt? Why was there only
shame and scorn, guilt and trouble? I wanted to
smash things, set them on fire, tear them apart with
my teeth, murder them! What are you lying and

whispering about behind my back? Why don't you say it straight to my face? I'll jump up from my desk, I'll climb on the rooftop, the stairs, the lobby. I'll push Chichkin aside and shout so that all can hear: Yes! Yes! Yes! I love her! Expel me, call the police, I don't give a damn! Yes, I belonged to a secret society! Yes, I kissed Anna Nikolayevna on Kalitnikovsky! Yes, I got D's last semester! Yes, I realize what I'm doing. What else?. . . Why are you tormenting her? Is it her fault that her fiancé died?. . . What if there is an age difference? Haven't you read *Jean Christophe*? Or Gorky's *Matvei Kozhemyakin*?. . . So what that she's a teacher? Aren't teachers human? Isn't she a woman?. . . Leave her alone, or I'll cut your throats!. . . I'll wait for you at night, Nose, and I don't know what I'll do to you. . . God, where is she now, what is she thinking? Why am I lying here instead of running to her, consoling her? I have to do something! But what? What?

. . . I'm sitting at the back entrance, frozen stiff, smoking my fifth cigarette, holding my ear to the smelly oilcloth, but she's still not there. I let her know that I'd come and would wait, I told her to come out. I'm shivering, my feet are blocks of ice, and there's a lump in my throat. I can't breathe, my temples are throbbing, and I have a headache. I haven't eaten in two days, I haven't been home, haven't been to school, I've been running wild in the streets, eating filthy snow, and I feel as if I have a temperature of 102. I'm crazed. The perfect time to lure me into a gang. I'd be ruthless and bold, with a gun under my arm, I knife in my boot. We rob a bank, a suitcase filled with roubles, two tickets to the Crimea, please, Anna Nikolayevna, come into our compartment, and what are you laughing at, fatface, the age difference amuses you? And how about my gun?. . . Let's run away from them all, the two of us, it's time to escape — and then time will tell. But how?. . . Where are you? Why aren't you coming? I know you're home. I know you feel bad too, come out, I can't live without you, we have to make a decision. I can't come up with a plan without you. Maybe you have one? I'll do whatever you say. But please. Just don't say those words: 'part', 'don't see each other', 'pretend'. There's no point in hiding or pretending, everyone knows. Thank God! What a relief! We have to walk down the street together, in front of everyone, laughing and kissing. Let them look. . . come out! I can't stand it! I'm going to start pounding and kicking that damn door and shout, 'Open up!'

Come out! come out!

But she's not there.

God, what if?. . . There's no way out! Why don't I free her and myself at once! Why all this fuss? 'There can't be anything between us, ever.' It's true. Are we supposed to get married? That's ridiculous!. . . Sanya's father has a gun, a small, nickel-plated Browning, a war trophy. It's like a toy. Last autumn we took the train to the woods, set up a tin can on a stump, and took turns shooting at it. Pow! Pow! The shots weren't loud, they were brief, and the handle fit in my hand. The trigger was easy. . . Pow! And it's over. I even know where Sanya keeps it: in Aunt Tamara's room. If I went through the room, I'd find it. How easy! There, you idiots, there's my answer to the age difference, to my empty pockets, to the cold, the D's, the secret societies which aren't secret and never will be and all your other 'nevers'. If never, then never. Pow! And it's over. And you, Anna Nikolayevna, you go on being afraid of all kinds of shitheads. You'll meet someone eventually. I'll free you. A young blond lieutenant colonel, happy and tall, with a Hero's Star, an Opel he brought back from the front, an apartment across the street from the main post office and a dacha on the river. 'Who insulted you, Anushka? The Nose? Ha-ha-ha!' He won't care. . . So stay happy, Anna Nikolayevna. Forgive me, mother, I have no way out. . .

Come on out, Anya, come out to me!

But she's not there.

'I didn't know a thing. . .'

'Of course. I had taken sick leave, I wasn't going out at all. I was also having trouble with my tooth, my cheek was so swollen and I just sat and cried. Lubov would run over after school. I'd have her bring packages to Mother at the hospital — but it was all too much. She's in the hospital, you'd disappeared, I've been fired, and my face is all crooked. A real holiday. It's true that misery loves company.'

'I didn't disappear, I. . .'

'Yes, I understand. Lubov said: he's gone and so's that Voka. I figured you were hanging around, going to movies. I ran out to the back landing a dozen times: you were never there.'

'I was.'

'I know you were, I could feel it. Well, Lubov would come over and tell me that all hell had broken loose at school. Some supported the Nose, and some Ivan Mikhailovich. The teachers said that it was scary going into the ninth grade, the kids were being dragged into the Komsomol regional office over your stupid society — didn't I tell you? But you didn't listen. Ivan Mikhailovich and the Nose got into an argument over me. He wouldn't sign my resignation. . . He came to see me, did you know?'

'Really?'

'Yes, he came. I was all weepy-eyed, in my bathrobe, with a bandaged cheek, it was horrible! He stalked and paced like a caged tiger. "Enough!" he shouted. "Forget it! We won't wash our dirty laundry in public!" '

'That's all they care about.'

'Don't be like that about him. The poor man was suffering, he didn't know how to ask me if it's true or not. He's a naive man, he simply can't imagine that I would. . . We've made such a mess! I told him that I wouldn't return to the school for anything. "If you don't go back, that means you're guilty," he said. "Then, consider me guilty. . ." The next day, Lubov came over, and I asked her what's new, and she says, "nothing!" End of the semester. Almost New Year. Vacation, everyone's crazy, no time to think of you. And she's in a rush, can't sit still for a minute. Imagine, it was like being hit over the head. It opened my eyes: that's just the way things are. I'm sitting around moping and bawling, and life's just going on: it's the end of the semester. So I stayed up till midnight, with my register, did my grades for the semester. I lost myself in my work a bit. "There," I thought, "that's the last time I'm giving you grades, kids," and I felt so sad that I couldn't even give Yagodkin the D he deserved.'

'You're kidding!'

'Honest! And then Lubov said to me: enough, shape up, let's celebrate the New Year like normal people. Why don't we go to Kotuar. We'll decorate a tree right in the middle of the woods, and so on. We'll ski, have fun, relax. . . But for some reason I don't like the idea of Kotuar. . .'

'Me neither.'

'Really? Why not?. . . Something went wrong there, didn't it?. . . Well, anyway, then I had an idea. Mother's in the hospital, Pavka and Slavka are spending their vacation with Aunt Olya in Kostroma, I'm all alone. . . Am I supposed to sit here in my bathrobe? No! The New Year is my favorite holiday, and I have to start my new life that day, enough of this!'

'Right.'

'Why not? And so I started washing and cleaning and asked Mikhailovich, the janitor, to buy me a tree and I went off to the steam bath and the beauty parlor. I even had a manicure. See? I waited in line for two hours. . . Lubov said that she and Gleb were going to a party, his fellow pilots — great, I thought I'd go with them. The swelling in my cheek had gone down completely. Pavka and Slavka left, before that we went together to visit Mama in the hospital, brought her cranberry pies that my neighbor Ivanovna had baked. Well, I thought, I'm alive! Alive!. . . And then I remembered my dress and thought, watch out world, here I come!. . . Do you like my dress?. . . What, are you stupid? You don't understand anything. This is an American dress, a real ball gown. I bought it at the flea market last year and haven't worn it since. . . You really are stupid! Look, I'm a real Lady Hamilton in it!. . .'

'What about me?'

'What about you? You were gone. Gone. And after I had made all these decisions, I called Tamara, to reach you. Can't I at least say good-bye to you?'

'Good-bye?'

'God! I got so involved with the duck I'm cooking and I was expecting you to ring the doorbell. And you didn't come and didn't come. It never occurred to me to look at the back door. And then I figured it out and I opened the door, God, how long had you been out there, you silly boy?'

She let me in the back way, and my hands wouldn't

bend, and my lips couldn't move from the cold. I couldn't even smile. It was so warm in the kitchen!. . . She didn't let me in, she dragged me in, hugged and squeezed me and started unbuttoning my coat for me, but I moved away: 'don't.'

That's because I didn't know whether it was her or not. Hair loose, arms bare to the shoulder, and the dress! Just like Deanna Durbin's: black velvet, down to the floor, and that thing, I don't know what it's called, over the shoulder. A clever dress, one shoulder bare while the whole dress seems to hang from the other.

They had told me she was sick. I pictured her in bed dying, but this! I had never seen her look so beautiful. In fact I had never seen a woman like that except in the movies. I thought she was waiting for someone else, a man. Her equal. Someone to match her clothes, her mood, this holiday, this night. And in came an icicle boy instead, a blue teenager.

Lubov and Gleb burst in. We didn't have time to exchange another word. I wanted to hide on the back stairs again, but she wouldn't let me and hid me in the bathroom. But it was no longer a bathroom — without the tub, with a black faucet for the water and an unused rusty shower head. There were crates, a barrel of sauerkraut, sacks, old shoes and buckets. I sat down on a stool and trembled. I could just hear their voices, because her room, I figured out, was farther down the hall, near the end. It was only at first, when Anna Nikolayevna had opened the door and let them in, having hidden me in here, that I heard them shouting loudly.

'Hurry up! We'll be late! The car's waiting! Get dressed!' ·

Gleb was laughing, he had been drinking already.

I understood it all. She hadn't been waiting for me. They were going somewhere . . . to celebrate the New Year. She wasn't sick. Her eyes were shiny, her shoulders were bare, she smelled of perfume. She didn't look like a miserable teacher, she looked like a queen. And I was in the way. I had waited two hours, like a fool. And now she would go away. Well, let her. At least we had seen each other. Where was she going? I wondered.

I thought that the guys are all at Sanya's, not talking about me.

At that moment I wanted to be there, with them.

Time was passing, it had to be at least eleven-twenty. They'd be late. She still had to let me out. Or maybe she wanted me to wait for her? And she'd come back in an hour or two. Well, the storeroom wasn't as warm as the kitchen, but it wasn't the back stairs either. Voices burst into the hallway, so loud that I jumped.

'But I promise, really!' Anna Nikolayevna was practically shouting. 'In one hour!'

'You won't find it,' Lubov said. 'How will you get there?'

'Don't worry! Go on, you'll be late!'

'No, Anya, tell me, tell me!' Gleb was shouting and laughing.

Was she really not going? So dressed up and adult,

with that hair, that dress? I thought she should go. What is there here for her with me?

'This is ridiculous!' Lubov said.

'Volodya's honking, hear him?' Gleb shouted.

'Lubov, I told you!' Anna Nikolayevna implored.

The conversation was by the entrance now and I could hear the door opening. The voices rolled out onto the stairwell, while here in the hallway, a new memorable voice appeared.

'So much noise! At least close the door, you barbarians!'

Oh no! I was trapped. I hoped the old woman wouldn't come for some sauerkraut — that barrel had to be hers.

Anna Nikolayevna was still talking on the stairs, then the door shut, things quietened down. She and the old woman talked ('Guests, were they?' 'Yes, Ivanovna, guests!'), and I heard Anna Nikolayevna's footsteps go past. She went back to her room.

I froze and waited. I couldn't get her dress and new look out of my head. I think I was intimidated.

Her steps again. No, past me. To the kitchen. Now she was coming back. I got up. No, past me again. . . I waited for the steps, but suddenly, as if she had flown through the air, the door opened. I saw a beckoning hand which took mine and led me away.

And I noticed it again: the way she beckoned, the way she took my hand so easily — it wasn't *our* way, not the way we did things, it was new.

And for the first time in my life I was in her room.

'Well, come in!'

I was blinded by the dark, the candles burning on the tree. I was enveloped by the warmth and smell of the old house, the pine, the coziness. Her home! Was I really there? And some woman, mad and beautiful, wrapped her bare arms around me, held me and started kissing me. I stood stock still, afraid to hug her, to respond, to touch her. Where was I? Who was this? What was this?. . .

An old-fashioned clock on the wall, its brass pendulum gleaming, struck the half hour.

'We're going to see the New Year in together. Do you want to?'

Honestly, I didn't recognize her. Her smiles, her shining eyes, her animation. It's true that people are different at home.

'Don't you have to go?'

'Me? Later. Maybe. Are you hungry?'

I couldn't believe it. She, in her own home, was asking me to eat. We were going to sit down at this table, eat, and see the New Year in. Alone? Without worrying about anyone? I kept expecting someone to come in, to say, 'What are you doing here, kid?'

She pulled off my coat, and I was standing there in a sweater with my white shirt collar sticking out over it. I was ashamed of my old, albeit ironed, trousers over my polished boots, my sweater and my red hands. The black window and the tree ornaments reflected a skinny boy with a scared face and a pathetic white collar. And behind him a hurrying Lady Hamilton moved and glowed, with her blond hair and bare arms, a woman with an unfamiliar smile, a brave voice and challenging bravado. She cast up the white tablecloth and it hit the table with a starched crunch. She clattered dishes, frightening me. And she talked, and talked, and talked. . .

'And so I washed and cleaned up, then asked Mikhailovich the janitor to buy me a tree. . . See the manicure?' And she lifted her hand up to my face with an unrestrained gesture that I had never seen before, turning the shining flame-like nails to me.

I could neither get over it nor could I get warmed up. It would have been better if she had thrown on her coat and come out to the back stairs with me.

She turned on the light briefly, and I shuddered. She asked me to turn on the record player, but the record's volume scared me. I didn't dare sit down or light a cigarette. And there wasn't a single book or magazine in the room to flip through, the way you do in a strange house.

She came in and out and talked with Ivanovna. I was afraid that the old woman would look in. The door was open revealing another small room. It was dark in there, but I could see a chair and the headboard of a bed. I guessed that it was Anna Nikolayevna's bedroom and that it was her bed.

Anna Nikolayevna came back just as quick and animated, brought in a tubby decanter filled with a dark liqueur and said she was sorry there was no champagne.

'Well? Pretty nice, no? Please sit down,' she said, spreading her arms over the table.

Her tone was almost swaggering. I was particularly embarrassed by those beautiful naked arms and the arm pits that were sometimes exposed. Her arms seemed incredibly long.

She didn't seem to be hurrying anywhere, but I kept thinking that she had promised to go out somewhere later.

We were having a real holiday. New Year's Eve — candles, white tablecloth, crystal glasses, 'Rio Rita' on the record player. I poured the liqueur, the old-fashioned hands on the clock were close to twelve.

'Well, why are you like this?' she asked.

And I didn't know. Instead of getting merrier, I was getting gloomier, and I didn't know what to do or say. I felt out of place. As if it weren't me sitting there. And, to my shame, I also thought that I hadn't brought her a present, not the teeniest thing.

'And so we'll say good-bye, you and I,' she said. She said it merrily, simply, offering me her glass across the table.

'What do you mean?' I stopped raising my glass toward hers. But I didn't look at her.

'Just that. We'll say good-bye and it'll be over. Come on, come on!'

I pretended that I wouldn't drink to that.

'Come on, I'm joking. To you, my sunshine! Happy New Year!'

The clock behind her struck twelve. We got up. Clinked glasses. I watched her empty her glass. She drank, laughed, sat down. I drank. The clock was still striking. She put her glass down hard, leaned back and began laughing. I didn't understand. She was laughing, but her lips were going awry and she kept biting them.

That's how our sad New Year began.

Then she had hysterics.

Afraid of Ivanovna, I ran to the kitchen for water, wet a towel and put it on her forehead. How she wept! She pulled at her hair, blew her nose in an ugly way into the towel, sobbed, tried to explain something.

I led her to the couch, sat down next to her, rubbed her ice-cold hands, shyly kissed her face, her wet eyes. She wanted to reply, but the tears wouldn't let her breathe, her teeth chattered.

'Anya! Darling! Anya, come on. . .'

I thought that I would stop her somehow, change her mood, so that she would stop crying. But I couldn't kiss her the way I used to, the way I always did. Not in this room, in this house. I didn't dare. Not a woman like that. In a dress like that.

Suddenly she turned, stopping me, held my neck, my head, and I heard her say:

'Dar . . . darling . . . my poor . . . my little . . . I . . . I. . .' She started bawling again, her teeth chattering, she couldn't speak.

I was completely turned off. I was frozen.

I wanted to sit back down at the table, just to talk with her. I would have even run off to the guys, that's how hard it was for me there.

I cringed: I buried my face in her stupid dress, she caressed my head, we were like brother and sister shattered by the same grief, and our miserable love fluttered above us in astonishment, not knowing what to do with itself.

The candles on the tree burned out one after the other, music and drunken songs came from below. Ivanovna walked down the hallway and flushed the toilet, and the clock ticked evenly. We were side by side, cooling off, like two people killed in one battle, in a black, black field.

We returned toward midnight, everyone was asleep. Mother and Aunt Raya in the living room on the landlady's bed, the landlady and kids on the Russian stove. Snores were coming from there. The big chest was also made up with bedding, the blanket turned back. Darya had been sleeping, but she let us in. She had heard the car, we didn't even knock. Uncle Volodya was draining the radiator of his truck, it was almost twenty below zero. We unloaded the potatoes, two sacks which we brought into the shed so they wouldn't freeze, and Darya lit the shed for us with a kerosene lamp, a shawl tossed over her head and shoulders and low boots on her feet. But she wasn't sleepy, she was cheerful and giggly, and as plump as a toy. I had forgotten about Darya during the long day but when I saw her slightly slanting eyes, her black shiny hair in a bedtime braid and her smile, I remembered right away: how we arrived, how Darya was walking from the well with two wooden buckets on a yoke, as if out of a Russian fairy-tale. She was so tubby that, from a distance, it looked as if there were three buckets floating on a yoke, a big one and two smaller ones.

We called what we were doing 'industrying': Mother and Aunt Raya took two or three days off and traveled with Uncle Volodya on one of his long hauls. He would drop them in some village to trade city rags for potatoes, butter, or meat, and then pick them up on the way back. You couldn't get too rich on village products then, but there were always potatoes.

The landlady here knew Uncle Volodya from last year, but she didn't have anything to barter or sell this time. Mother and Aunt Raya decided to stay on anyway and go to other houses from there. Uncle Volodya was in a hurry to deliver his freight, and I went with him to the village of Vekovye, and along the way we 'industried' a bit more and came back with some potatoes.

I remembered how we had arrived, got warm, had a meal and drank wild cherry tea. The landlady kept complaining and whining: she was sick, and she had no cattle, and the kids were in rags and there were only six men left in the whole village, and one of them had lost a leg and another was blind. And Darya — I never did understand whether she was a daughter or a relative, with her non-Russian eyes and black hair (her name must have been Dariya, but everyone said Darya, and there was something exotic about that too) — was the physical opposite of the landlady. She had a shining round face. She rolled around like a ball, laughing, her eyes flashing. Her teeth were extraordinary: two full rows of strong solid teeth, like rows of corn. And she went in and out of the house, fetching wood or water, feeding the pigs and chickens. Then the kids came home from school, two boys. She carried things back and forth from the table. 'Enough complaining, we're alive!' she said to the landlady. 'Why is he so frail?' she laughed at me. 'Look at his little hands!' And with her calloused, short-fingered hand she took mine and laughed, turning them over. I almost blushed at how white and smooth they were. 'Leave him here with us, we'll shape him up!'

We had left in the daytime, the kids clinging to the truck, and two old women and three village girls (one pretty, in a white shawl) came to wave good-bye. Darya had run out onto the porch in a jacket and with nothing on her head. She must have said something about me to the girls: they laughed, but I was already in the cab and couldn't hear. I waved through the glass, but then I never gave her another thought.

Now we were frozen through and hungry. Uncle Volodya had half a bottle of moonshine left from the other village. We had hoped to sit around and eat with everyone, but they were asleep. Aunt Raya came out all sleepy and yawning like a hippo — where had we been so long and what did we want to eat? She had just fallen asleep.

'Go to bed,' Darya said, 'I'll feed them.'

We were warming our hands and backs against the stove and smiling with wooden lips. We described how we had bought the potatoes, how we got stuck in a drift, but Aunt Raya wasn't listening. She yawned and went to bed. Darya carried things to the table past us: a kettle of soup out of the stove, a tea pot, a bowl of cabbage, glasses, onions, bread. She didn't sit with us, but went back to her chest and watched us from her pillows and laughed. The light from the table didn't quite reach that far, and I could only see Darya's eyes shining.

Uncle Volodya was too tired to do justice to the soup, but I was waking up, even though I had been sleepy in the truck. I went out for a smoke twice, standing in complete darkness except for the glowing tip of my cigarette, thinking that it was only January fourth.

I kept seeing the roads, the snowy white fields amid the wintery forests, the fir branches covered with snow, naked shivering birches, other oncoming cars and deserted cold villages — only the smoke coming out of the chimneys showed that they were inhabited. At one point a passenger train traveled next to us for a while. I saw people in the restaurant car at tables and they saw me.

Only a day had gone by, twenty-four hours, since Mother and I had got up before dark and set out, but it felt so long ago. Everything that I had lived for, everything that I had had and that had happened to me seemed part of the distant past.

I couldn't even think. There was nothing, had

been nothing; only this hut, its entrance smelling of hay and rotten apples. I went out to relieve myself, and the night was black without moon or stars. It was unbelievably silent. Was there a city somewhere in the world, with streets, schools, theaters, teachers? The cold took the warmth out of my clothing in half a minute and then got inside: cold, night, nothing else, except that strange Darya inside on the chest. That was all.

A bed had been laid for me between the stove and the log wall, behind a curtain. It was on a wooden cot that you could climb into only from the foot ('That's Grandad's place, there, we buried him last spring'), and it was piled with cushions and pillows and small blankets. The cot listed down at the head but it was wide and cozy, my own little cave. It felt like climbing into a closet or crate and feeling that you had a secret private place. I undressed there, as if in a railway berth, put the clothes under my pillow and placed my boots outside. The lamp was still glowing on the table, which had not been cleared of the kettle, the bowls and the empty bottle. Snores filled the hut from every corner, the clock ticked, a child on the stove bed whimpered and ground his teeth. I looked in the direction of the chest and saw nothing. Had Darya pulled the covers over her head? But when I settled down, bare feet scampered over the floor, the lamp was blown out — I froze — and then I smelled the kerosene burn, and that was that. Quiet and dark.

Grandad's old corner smelled foreign, of shag

tobacco, sheep, and straw. I patted the stove's side and picked at bits of the whitewash. I was tense, waiting for something. Fear rounded my eyes in the dark. What was I waiting for? I looked and saw nothing, listened and heard nothing. But the tension was unbearable.

Quiet! Suddenly bare feet padded firmly across the floor. Where to? Almost to the door, to the corner. The buckets of water were kept there. I heard a cup splash.

'Oh, I'm so thirsty,' said Darya to herself. 'All that city herring!'

I heard the water going down her throat.

Was it me? No, it was not me who quickly sat up and pulled back the curtain. The window was white with snowy light. I could make out objects on the table, the stove to one side, and right in front of me, an unclear nocturnal figure.

'Ooh, what do you want?' she asked in a whisper, even though she hadn't been whispering before.

'A smoke.' My voice was unsteady.

There was a brief silence.

'Don't go, smoke here, smoky!'

I had already put my bare feet on the floor, feeling for my boots.

'I'm just drinking and drinking!. . . Sleep! Why aren't you sleeping? You're not sleeping and you're not letting anyone else sleep either. . .'

'Me?'

'Well, it's not me!. . . Need a match?'

'Yes please, there's a box on the table. . .'

She stepped over to the table and then came over to me, her hand extended. She blocked the window, the hut, she was close, so close I could smell her night-time warmth, her bed smell. Our hands met, she was handing me a cigarette and the matchbox, but I didn't take them right away, afraid to drop them. I extended my other hand, and she took it by the wrist with her other hand so that she could place the cigarette and matches in my palm. Fat, calloused fingers, clumsy tenderness, unfamiliar.

'Mister Whitehands, you have to wait on him,' she laughed in a whisper and moved even closer, so close that the soft and warm fabric of her nightshirt touched my knees.

'Sleep! Why aren't you asleep?'

And she held my wrist in her strong hand.

Ladislav Fuks

THE CREMATOR

Translated by Eva M. Kandler

The eccentric Mr Kopfkringl enjoys his work in the Prague crematorium. He is proud of his expertise in the mechanics of incineration and the social usefulness of his calling. He takes a mystical satisfaction in the speedy despatch of the dead 'into the ether', thus, he believes, hastening their journey toward reincarnation. In off-duty hours he expounds the humanitarian mysteries of cremation to family and friends, rereads his treasured volume on Tibet and coos patronizingly over his beautiful wife and children.

In *The Cremator*, leading Czech author Ladislav Fuks (born in 1923) has written a brooding black comedy on one man's trajectory towards Fascism. Set in 1939, just before and after the Nazi occupation of Czechoslovakia, the novel skillfully interweaves fantasy and reality, constructing its powerful story through elaborate detail and repeated, increasingly sinister motifs. Fuks is an incomparable writer whose work deserves wider recognition in the English-speaking world. His first book, *Mr Theodore Mundstock*, was published in Britain in 1969. A Czech film based on *The Cremator* was released in 1970.

Eva M. Kandler was born in Nottingham and educated in Prague. She is a graduate of Girton College and has previously translated prose and poetry and scientific papers from Czech and German. She currently lives in Oxford.

Vasily Shukshin

ROUBLES IN WORDS, KOPEKS IN FIGURES AND OTHER STORIES

Introduction by Yevgeny Yevtushenko

Translated from the Russian by
Natasha Ward and David Iliffe

When Vasily Shukshin died in 1974, tens of thousands of ordinary Russians attended his funeral. So popular was he, as actor, film director and writer, that even his enemies in the Soviet Bureaucracy felt compelled to make an appearance.

But what did the bureaucrats find so subversive in his work? Perhaps it was Shukshin's sharply observed but understated tales of peasant life and his unwillingness to adopt any ideological position vis a vis his subjects — he allowed them to speak for themselves, providing an insight into what ordinary people feel and experience in the Soviet Union today, where everyday concerns have changed little since the nineteenth century.

This collection of Shukshin's stories is introduced with a survey of his career by the celebrated Russian poet Yevgeny Yevtushenko.

Natasha Ward has translated books on the Arts into English as well as Bulgakov and some Yevtushenko poetry.

David Iliffe has translated the acting edition of Chekov's *The Seagull* (Samuel French) as well as *The Cherry Orchard, Uncle Vanya* and *The Three Sisters*.

Bella Akhmadulina

THE GARDEN

Edited, translated and introduced by F.D. Reeve
Bilingual Edition

Bella Akhmadulina stands out among contemporary Russian poets for her broad range, firm technique and spiritual vision. Celebrated for the originality and independence of her voice, her primary concern remains the power of language and the imagination.

This collection opens with the title poem of her Russian 1987 collection *The Garden* and includes many poems not previously published in English. It draws on the whole body of her work.

Bella Akhmadulina lives in Moscow and gives readings throughout the Soviet Union and in the United States and Europe. She was awarded the State Prize for literature in 1989.

Nika Turbina

FIRST DRAFT

Poems/Bilingual Text
Translations by Antonina W. Bouis
and Elaine Feinstein
Introduction by Yevgeny Yevtushenko

The poems in *First Draft* by Nika Turbina, a Russian child prodigy, show an astonishing awareness and lyricism and a very individual freshness and insight. They are moving, passionate and exquisitely wrought.

Nika Turbina was born in 1974 and still lives in Yalta. She is a celebrated poet in the USSR and received rapturous receptions when she recited her work in Europe and the USA. This collection was the winner of the prestigious Golden Lion of Venice prize.

'Turbina will receive more and more attention as the years go by. This serious little girl is likely someday to have an enormous influence.'   *People Magazine, USA*

Yevgeny Yevtushenko

THE FACE BEHIND THE FACE

Translated by Arthur Boyars and Simon Franklin

Yevgeny Yevtushenko's *The Face Behind the Face*, the latest and longest selection of work, is his own choice of poems written and published between 1972 and 1975. The book falls into six parts of which the first five sections are arranged thematically, and are taken from the 1975 volume, *A Father's Ear*. The sixth — a long poem *Snow in Tokyo* — first appeared in a Russian magazine in 1975. The version translated is from the two-volume Selected Works edition published in Russia in 1976.

'These poems beat and tumble and thrash with life, not the poet's or Russian life in particular, but our own as we hurtle or totter along. . .'   *Daily Telegraph*

'His real virtue, now as formerly, lies in the sudden twist of perception, the change of tone whereby he seizes upon an "ordinary" moment and opens up its hidden potential.'
                                                                               The Guardian

Yevgeny Yevtushenko

EARLY POEMS

Revised and Enlarged Bilingual Edition
Selected, edited and translated by George Reavey

This paperback re-issue of Yevgeny Yevtushenko's early poems collects the Russian poet's best work from 1953 — when he was twenty — to 1967. It includes some of his most famous work: *Babii Yar* (which forms the centrepiece of Shostakovich's Thirteenth Symphony), *Zima Station*, *The City of 'Yes' and the City of 'No'*, and *The Heirs of Stalin*, which he still reads to enormous acclaim at his brilliant recitals.

Yevgeny Yevtushenko, who has written a special preface for this re-issue, was born in Siberia in 1933 and now lives in Moscow. Hailed by *Time Magazine* as 'the Soviet superbard', he has also written two novels and has acted in and directed a number of films.